THE DOCTOR HAD A DOUBLE

THE DOCTOR HAD A DOUBLE

Claire Vernon

Chivers Press · Thorndike Press
Bath, England   Waterville, Maine USA

This Large Print edition is published by Chivers Press, England, and by Thorndike Press, USA.

Published in 2002 in the U.K. by arrangement with the author.

Published in 2002 in the U.S. by arrangement with Juliet Burton Literary Agency.

U.K. Hardcover ISBN 0–7540–4834–9 (Chivers Large Print)
U.S. Softcover   ISBN 0–7862–3938–7 (Nightingale Series Edition)

The text of this Large Print edition is unabridged.
Other aspects of the book may vary from the original edition.

Set in 16 pt. New Times Roman.

Printed in Great Britain on acid-free paper.

British Library Cataloguing in Publication Data available

Library of Congress Cataloging-in-Publication Data

Vernon, Claire.
     The doctor had a double / by Claire Vernon.
        p. cm.
     ISBN 0–7862–3938–7 (lg. print : sc : alk. paper)
     1. Physicians—Fiction. 2. Amsterdam (Netherlands)—Fiction.
     3. Twins—Fiction. 4. Large type books. I. Title.
     PR6072.E735 D58 2002
     823'.914—dc21   2001058473

CHAPTER ONE

Cherry Corfield looked up as the doctor's surgery door opened, and then she relaxed as she saw he was escorting his last patient to the door.

A rather special patient, Mrs. Chester. A little old lady, bent as she battled along leaning on her two sticks, she insisted on going out come rain or sunshine and was incredibly independent. She had the most contented face Cherry had ever seen.

Dr. Simon Britten was saying: 'Try not to overdo things, Mrs. Chester.'

The doctor was a tall thin man with short blond hair and sideburns that hardly showed.

How could he be so stupid, Cherry thought angrily. As if the poor old girl had any choice. A widow and childless with no relations alive.

Mrs. Chester was smiling up at him. 'Happen I don't want to be careful, Doctor? I like living my way. I'm nearer eighty than you'll ever be.' She chuckled. 'Fresh air and exercise, that's my recipe.'

'I just want to keep you out of hospital.'

She laughed, shaking her head. 'Fair created, didn't I? Never had so much fun in my life. Happen I'll never see anyone look so shocked as the Sister when I threw the cold soup over her.'

'That wasn't a very nice thing to do,' the doctor scolded gently.

Mrs. Chester laughed. ' 'Twasn't intended to be. I wanted her to see how cold the soup was. She wouldn't believe me but she did . . . afterwards!'

'You really are the limit,' the doctor said, laughing and trying to ease her tactfully out of the door.

Finally she went and he closed the door, putting down the lock. Yawning, stretching his arms, he walked down the lofty hall of the old terrace house towards the receptionist.

'A letter for you, Dr. Britten,' she said, holding out an envelope.

He took it, a little startled by the unexpected animosity in her voice.

It was a coldness he was not accustomed to in girls' voices, or in anyone's, for that matter, for Simon Britten was a quiet pleasant man, dedicated to his work, a contented bachelor, who seemed able to get on well with everyone.

He stared at the girl and saw her, perhaps for the first time, because before he had been too busy to see she was, what his friend Paul would have called: 'a dish'.

Now Simon saw that although she looked absurdly young—as all girls did these days—he knew she was about thirty. She had short curly red hair, green eyes and freckles on her tip-tilted nose. Her mouth was a thin line of disapproval and there was a cold hatred in her

2

eyes that shook him.

He took the letter, remembering the discussion his group of doctors had had before they engaged Cherry Corfield. No one could understand why a girl with such excellent references and varied experience and who was also a good linguist would want the job of doctors' receptionist in a quiet seaside town like Hastings. However, they had taken her for she was the best of the applications.

Glancing at the envelope, he recognised the spidery but elegant writing. 'Oh, no!' he said without thinking. 'Aunt Flo. Hell. I should have written to her.'

'It's easy to forget people. Particularly old ones,' Cherry told him.

Simon pulled up a chair, swung it round and straddled it, slitting open the envelope.

'All the same, that's no excuse,' he said. 'I owe my Aunt Flo so much. My mother died when I was a baby and though Aunt Flo was pretty old then—she must be at least seventy-eight today!—that makes her forty-three when she got landed with me, she was wonderful.'

'And your father?'

Simon pulled out several sheets of thin paper and smoothed them. He didn't look up. 'Oh, he went off to Australia when I was a baby. He kept me, educated me but never wrote to me. He died last year. It didn't mean a thing.'

'Does anything?' Cherry asked bitterly but

Simon didn't hear. He read the letter. Then he looked up, his face startled.

'Just listen to this,' he said and read aloud. 'Dear boy, I wonder if you would do me a favour. Every year I go over to Amsterdam to see the bulbs in their beauty. This year my doctor has advised me not to travel alone. Personally I think it is a lot of nonsense but he seems to think my blood pressure is up and as he points out, I am no chicken. I only go for a night or two, dear boy, so I wondered if you would escort me? I know how busy you must be but it would be such a help. Naturally I insist that you be my guest. You can buy me a brandy on the plane, dear boy, for I find that soothes my agitated tummy. I am always nervous flying but it is so much simpler and far less exhausting than by ship and train. I am enclosing a list of dates available and perhaps you would get your secretary to ring me back and tell me which suits you best . . .' he read. 'Well, I'll be . . .' Simon put the letter on the desk and looked at the silent girl.

'I ask you! Careering round the world at the age of seventy-eight.'

'Why not?' Cherry asked coldly. 'Surely even the old are entitled to enjoy themselves.'

It might have been her voice or could have been the words that surprised him. 'Of course they are,' he said puzzled. 'Is that the impression you get from me? That I don't think they should enjoy themselves.'

4

She shrugged. She was well and, as Paul would say, pleasantly built. Her frock was navy blue with a white collar and cuffs and she had a white cardigan slung round her shoulders.

'Personally I don't think you care,' she said.

'You don't?' He was even more startled. 'What makes you think that?'

'Your complete indifference, Dr. Britten.' she said stiffly. 'That old Mrs. Chester. The way you shooed her out and then sat down here with plenty of time to spare. Don't you realise that she lives alone and that probably you are the only person she will have to talk to today? That's why half these old dears keep coming to the doctor or sending for help, because they go nearly mad with loneliness and the need to speak to someone, just anyone, even if he doesn't care about them.

'Then . . .' she went on, her voice rising angrily, lifting her hand as he tried to interrupt. 'Then take your aunt's letter. She asks you to let your secretary phone her. Why not you? Because you are too busy.' She gave a little snort. 'Busy my foot. You waste half your time losing things. I've never worked for anyone so careless, so undisciplined, so utterly helpless. The trouble is you've been spoilt . . .'

She had to pause for breath then, and sat very still.

'Well,' Simon said slowly. 'That was a mouthful. Feel better for it?'

Startled by his gentle reply, she went bright

5

red. 'Yes,' she admitted. 'I apologise.'

'Please don't.' Simon leant forward, frowning a little as he stared at her. 'It does one's ego good to hear a few home truths. Is that how I appear to you? Indifferent, untidy, spoiled, unfeeling?'

Her cheeks burned even more. 'Well, er . . . in a way . . .'

'I probably am, you know,' he said thoughtfully. 'I think Aunt Flo did spoil me, now I come to think of it, and of course, here, Mrs. Edwards spoils me.'

'They all spoil you,' Cherry said, once again aggressive.

'Is that such a bad thing?' Simon asked, his voice thoughtful. 'Could it be that you are jealous? I mean of my being spoilt,' he added hastily. 'It sounds to me as if you lack security . . . as if you need loving, being cherished . . .' he stopped abruptly for Cherry had stood up, knocking over her chair noisily, looking at him angrily, the tears coming out of her green eyes.

'I hate you,' she said and turned, running for the small cloakroom behind the stairs.

Simon stood up. He shrugged. Women! Funny creatures.

Going back to his surgery, Simon re-read the letter and then picked up the phone. He soon heard Aunt Flo's quavery voice.

'Dear boy, how very sweet of you to phone,' she said. 'It is so lovely hearing your voice. And so clear. Just as if you were by my side. I

6

hope you didn't mind me asking you?'

'Mind?' he answered and laughed. 'I felt flattered. I'm a lousy nephew, Aunt Flo, and I'm sorry.'

'Dear boy.' She sounded shocked. 'Such nonsense. You are a good nephew. You never forget my birthday or Christmas and you write . . .'

'Occasionally,' he said dryly.

'Well, dear boy, you're only like all men. Your father was even worse than you and so was my father. Men are hopeless writers and until women recognise and accept this, there is much heartbreak. I don't think letters mean as much to men as they do to women. We read them again and again, even keep them and read them perhaps fifty years later.' She laughed. A fragile sort of laugh. 'Love is a different thing where women are concerned, dear boy. No girl friends?' she asked, almost wistfully.

'Not at the moment.' He laughed. 'Maybe we'd better get down to business. The twenty-fourth would suit me best. I've got some days off coming.'

'Dear boy, how wonderful. That would suit me, too. Oh, I am looking forward to it and seeing you, too, of course.'

'Your doctor thinks it's all right for you to go?'

'Oh yes, but not alone. It makes such a difference when you have an escort.'

7

Again he felt guilt. How often had he even thought of Aunt Flo, living all alone in Brighton? She was so near yet rarely did he see her. Cherry Corfield was right, he was a selfish spoiled brute.

'I'll drive over and fetch you . . .'

'Oh no, dear boy, I have a good man here who has a taxi service. He takes me to Gatwick at a very easy rate and is such a good driver. I can relax so perfectly with him . . .'

Simon grinned wryly, remembering the time he had driven Aunt Flo to Rye and had been involved in a car accident. Not his fault. Fortunately no one was hurt but Aunt Flo had a nasty shock and though she never complained or reprimanded him, he had noticed that if he suggested a car ride, on the rare occasions he saw her, she always very tactfully got out of it.

'Dear boy, I'll let you know what time to be at Gatwick. We have to be there an hour before we fly, you know. It'll only be one night so you needn't have much luggage. Oh, dear boy, you have made me so happy . . .' Her voice was unsteady for a moment but then normal again. 'I won't keep you, but it has been so nice hearing your voice.'

He put down the receiver slowly and sat back in his swivel chair. Whew. What a heel he'd been. Unintentionally too. Not that that was an excuse, by any means. but somehow the days flew by and you forgot . . .

8

'It was easy to forget people,' Cherry Corfield had said.

Had someone forgotten her?

CHAPTER TWO

Everything went wrong on the day of the trip to Amsterdam. Simon planned to rise early but overslept. He was rushed to the station by Paul Donward, one of the other doctors, a friendly, fat greying man who always joked, for Simon's car was in the garage with some unknown fault. Luckily the train before Simon's was late so he managed to catch his own.

It was a cold day and he was glad of an overcoat and gloves. Together with an umbrella it made him a typical English man, he thought, glancing in the hall mirror before he left.

'Most handsome,' Cherry Corfield said dryly as she passed him to answer the phone.

He looked at her and smiled. After the small explosion in which she had rushed from the room, shouting she hated him, he had done his best to avoid being alone with her. He had behaved normally and completely ignored the little angry scene, hoping she would also be able to forget it.

As he hurried up the stairs from the station at Gatwick Airport and wondered where he'd find his Aunt Flo. he wondered if he had been wise. Would Cherry Corfield perhaps see his avoidance of her as indifference and make her hate him even more? He didn't like being hated! Especially by her.

It was a strange experience. The first time he had fallen for a girl who hated him! Also who made it plain that she did so!

Pausing with shock, Simon realised what he had just thought.

Fallen for a girl . . . ?

Had he fallen for Cherry Corfield? Why, he hardly knew her. Until that day of the row, he had barely spoken more than a dozen words at a time to her. He didn't believe in mixing love with work and so avoided looking at the receptionists in such a way. True, he thought with a sudden smile, most of them were rather aged or unattractive. Cherry was the prettiest they had ever had.

Yet it wasn't her looks. There was something about her that fascinated him. Something that made him feel sorry for her and want to help her one moment; and the next to know she was capable of hurting him if he let her. In any case, it couldn't be her looks, for he hadn't even noticed her properly until that day when she had spoken with such cold *hatred* in her voice that he had been startled.

He looked round worriedly. No sign of Aunt Flo. Perhaps her hired car had broken down. He went to the counter and got his ticket, sailed through past the Passport counter and then saw Aunt Flo.

She was sitting patiently in the Reception Lounge. A small fragile-like woman with a long thin face, white hair, half-hidden by a violet cloche, wearing a long matching coat. She sat very still, hands folded demurely on her lap, an overnight airways bag on the ground by her side.

'Aunt Flo . . .' he said affectionately, hurrying to her side. Half-lifting her from her seat, he kissed her.

'Dear boy . . .' Aunt Flo's pale thin face brightened the rose colour returning to her cheeks.

'I am sorry I'm late. The train was . . .'

'Never mind, dear boy. You were never one for punctuality.' There was an elf-like mischievousness in Aunt Flo's eyes. 'Would you get us a cup of coffee each? We've got another forty minutes but I like to start walking to our place early, otherwise you don't get a good seat.'

Simon hurried to the counter, queueing up but finally getting two cups of coffee, a huge cheese sandwich for himself and a small chocolate cake for Aunt Flo.

Everywhere was crowded, a constant movement of people. The husky attractive voices of the receptionists came over the tannoy with a regularity you grew accustomed to, each announcement being followed by a

11

flow of passengers as they made their way to their waiting plane.

Sitting by Aunt Flo's side, drinking coffee, eating hungrily for he'd had no proper breakfast, Simon watched the people hurrying by.

'You're an old hand at this,' he teased Aunt Flo.

She was wiping her fingers daintily on a tissue.

'That cake was delicious but I have to watch my weight dear boy.' She saw his quick concerned glance at her skeleton-like figure and chuckled. 'I don't stay thin like this by accident, dear boy. It requires self-discipline and sacrifice.'

'But why bother . . .' Simon began and stopped feeling his cheeks hot.

He had nearly said *at your age*. How tactless could one be? 'I mean, Aunt Flo, you always *were* thin. I can't see you putting on weight and you might as well enjoy life.'

She chuckled. 'While I have it. Dear boy, I am only seventy-eight. Most of my friends are in their late eighties, some are over ninety. I don't want to get fat for my clothes won't fit me and that would be a disaster.'

A quiet husky voice called their number. They stood up and walked along the glass-walled corridors until they came to their deck and the steps. Already a queue was forming.

'You sit down, Aunt Flo, and I'll keep your

place,' Simon said.

She beamed. 'How sweet of you, dear, but I think I'd rather stand. I like to choose my own seat on the plane.'

Slowly they moved down the steps and then handed over the boarding tickets they'd been given. He watched the quick determined way Aunt Flo climbed the stairs and then walked down the aisle until she came to a seat.

'Ah, my lucky number,' she said happily, moving in, sitting by the small window.

Simon settled by her side. He had done quite a lot of flying and it never disturbed him but he saw the way she kept clenching and unclenching her hand and made a note that he must talk to her about something that would interest her when the time for take-off came.

The plane was filling up, the seats occupied, the hostesses going up and down the aisle, seeing everyone had put out their cigarettes and done up their belts.

'What a pretty girl,' Aunt Flo said as a tall, gracefully slender hostess, with dark hair showing under her gay little cap, walked by.

'Pretty?' Simon looked down the aisle at the girl. 'Good legs, yes,' he added but she wasn't half as attractive as Cherry.

'Are you going to be a bachelor all your life, Simon?' Aunt Flo asked.

Her hand was busily engaged in clenching and unclenching for the engines were making their satanic roar and the plane began to move round as it would move for what seemed like hours and still be on the ground.

Simon closed his hand over hers and turned to smile at her.

'Frankly, Aunt Flo, I don't know. I've been in and out of love a number of times but marriage is pretty . . . well . . .' He laughed. 'It makes such a difference to a man's life.'

'And a woman's,' she said quietly.

He looked at her. 'Why didn't you marry, Aunt Flo? You were a very pretty girl. I know by your album.'

'I had to nurse my mother, dear boy. Then poor Dad and by the time they'd passed on, I was forty and then . . .'

'Then I came along. I am sorry.'

She smiled. 'Don't be, dear boy. No, actually, it was your mother, my young sister. After she had . . . had you, she was very delicate and needed nursing so I moved in. At your father's request. He hadn't much patience with illness, you know. The sort of man who says "Pull your socks up" or "stop fussing". Yet let him have a cold or a pain, and there was murder, demands for immediate attention. Men are queer cattle . . .' she said, her smile taking the sting that might have been in the words.

'Then your mother got worse and worse and finally died and I . . . well. I just stayed on. We lived in a very nice house in Carbis Bay on the Cornish coast. Then . . . then one day your

14

father announced that he was going to emigrate to Australia. He said he'd take . . . As I've told you before, he said he thought it wiser not to take you, Simon dear, not because he didn't love you,' she added hastily, 'But you were a very delicate baby. You kept getting bronchitis. He said he didn't think it a good idea. Neither did I.'

She smiled at him, her fingers curled round his. 'You were the joy of my life, dear boy. The answer to my prayers. You were the child I could never have and I was so happy.'

'But you must have found me rather a bind.'

Simon glanced out of the window and saw they were off the ground already, the busy neighbourhood they had just left had turned into what looked like squares of strange colours. The massive fluffy clouds were below and round the plane.

The impersonal voice told them it was the Captain speaking and he welcomed them all and now they could undo their seat belts if they liked but he would prefer them to leave them done up, but loosely, as the clouds suggested they might have a slight unevenness for a while but not to worry.

'Are we up?' Aunt Flo asked, startled.

'Yes. Fast, wasn't it?'

She peered through the window. 'My word we are.' She turned to beam at Simon. 'I've never had such a pleasant take-off. I wasn't a bit nervous. Thank you so much, dear boy.'

15

Simon beckoned the other hostess, an equally pretty girl with blonde hair and a big smile but not a patch as compared with Cherry . . . He cursed silently. Cherry was getting too much in his thoughts. It was absurd. He didn't even know her.

'Two brandies please,' he said, 'and tonic water.'

He turned back to Aunt Flo. 'I was asking you if you didn't find me rather a bind. I mean, you were all of forty-three and landed with a delicate child.'

'Ah, but don't you see, dear boy, you were the answer to my prayers. I had always had someone to love, to cherish, perhaps to spoil. First my dear mother, then poor Dad, then sweet Angela, your mother, and then you. What more could a woman want?'

'Did you miss me when I went to school?'

The plane was bouncing around and some of the passengers were laughing and joking about it but Aunt Flo showed no sign of anxiety.

'Terribly, dear boy, terribly.'

'But you've always been so good. So unpossessive.'

She smiled. 'We have our children for so short a while that we must make the most of it. Then they leave home and we must undo the strings that tied them to us. It hurts terribly, dear boy, but if we cling to our children, we may end up by being hated, or we may ruin our

16

children's lives.'

'You are so right, you know,' Simon said thoughtfully. 'So many of my friends have had that to cope with. The fear of hurting, yet the impossibility of going on living at home and being treated like a four year old, with someone fussing if you are late or not eating enough.' He laughed. 'You were the sensible one.'

The hostess arrived with the tiny bottles of brandy, the bigger bottles of tonic and two glasses.

He watched her walk down the aisle again. She hadn't as graceful a walk as Cherry . . .

Cherry, again! He felt annoyed and turned to talk to Aunt Flo again in order to forget the wretched girl. But he couldn't.

The landing was perfect, hardly any bump felt, and then there was the long slow walk through the wind and into the airport building. As he walked along with Aunt Flo, a long queue of people passed, hurrying, carrying their overnight bags or handbags.

A man leapt over the rail that divided the two lanes of walking, grabbed Simon's arm and grinned.

'Bit of a change, man . . .' he said and looked at Aunt Flo, then lifted his hand. 'Be seeing you . . .' he added and was gone, a tall man in a light macintosh, and a big red moustache and dark glasses.

'Who was that?' Aunt Flo asked.

Simon looked as puzzled as he felt 'I haven't a clue. Never seen the man in my life before.'

'What a strange thing he said . . .' Aunt Flo went on.

Soon they were through the usual formalities and outside, climbing into the waiting coach, their courier telling them where they were going. First it would be in a glass-roofed barge round the canals.

'I always enjoy that,' Aunt Flo said later, sitting down by the large window in the barge. 'The canals are fascinating and the bridges too. We go right out in the harbour. I hope you are a good sailor, dear boy, for it can be a bit rough.' She chuckled.

Simon stared at her. She was really enjoying it, he saw. She talked away, pointing out the large number of bicycles, and the precarious way the cars were parked near the edge of the canals.

'Sometimes they slide in,' she chuckled. 'So I'm told. You have to watch out. Aren't the bridges fascinating?'

He might have said they were not for he had a strange feeling that he should not be there. That he was wasting his time. Losing an opportunity.

An opportunity for what? he asked himself. If only he could get that girl out of his thoughts!

Now as he listened to the middle-aged and elderly women, a few with husbands, around him chattering, he wondered if they really enjoyed the trip or if it was just a chance to see people and talk. His own life was so full that he had never thought of the need of that.

'Isn't the courier pretty?' Aunt Flo asked almost wistfully. 'It seems so strange to me, dear boy, that you aren't lonely.'

Simon laughed. 'I haven't time to be. I live where we have our surgeries and there is a good housekeeper, in her late fifties, I hasten to add,' he teased with a smile, 'who spoils me completely. At least so I was told the other day. That I was undisciplined, untidy, thoughtless and spoiled.'

The barge was going out into the harbour. A huge white liner stood, towering above them.

Aunt Flo looked shocked. 'Whoever would say such a wicked thing?'

'Maybe it is true, Aunt Flo. You certainly spoiled me.' Simon smiled at her. 'You were a wonderful mother, you know.'

Her cheeks went red and her eyes filled with tears.

'Dear boy, you always were a darling. But who said such nasty things about you?' she asked sharply. She had always been quick to defend him, he remembered.

'Just a girl,' he said casually and began to wish he hadn't mentioned her. Aunt Flo had an uncanny habit of reading thoughts.

Now she looked at him curiously. 'Just . . .?'

19

He fidgeted a little. 'I hardly know her.'

Aunt Flo put her head on one side. 'There always has to be a start somewhere. Is she pretty?'

'Aunt Flo, you're incorrigible,' Simon burst out laughing.

His aunt wagged her finger at him. 'I remember when you first learned that word, Simon. You were a small boy and so proud of it. For days everything that happened was *incowwigable.*'

They laughed and Simon felt glad they had left the subject of a possible girl friend. Aunt Flo had always been a matchmaker but recently she seemed to have given up all hope. But she hadn't forgotten!

'What colour hair has she?' she asked casually, leaning forward to look at the warehouses on the island. 'What a fascinating place this is and what courage the Dutch have. Built out of water, this was. D'you remember me telling you the story of the little Dutch boy who stood with his finger pressed against the hole? How you loved being told stories,' she laughed gently. 'What was the colour of her hair, dear boy?'

'Red,' he said without thinking and then started at her. 'Aunt Flo, none of your tricks.'

She laughed again. 'It's so nice to know you even notice a girl. You'll make a good husband and father, dear boy.'

'I'm sure Cherry doesn't think so,' he said

before he realised it.

'Why not? What has she against you?'

Giving up, Simon told her the whole story. Starting with the old Mrs. Chester and her behaviour at the hospital which made Aunt Flo laugh until she nearly cried and then Cherry's sudden outburst.

'It looks to me,' Simon finished, 'as if some man has badly hurt the girl so she hates the lot of us.'

'So you must walk warily,' Aunt Flo said.

'That's what I . . .' Simon began, then turned to look at his aunt. 'You should be in the C.I.D. Aunt Flo,' he said, laughing. 'You have a diabolical method of making your victim talk.'

Later as they were getting into the coach again, a man on a bicycle going past waved.

'Be seeing you,' he shouted.

Simon, about to get on the coach, looked round. But no one behind him was taking any notice of the cyclist. *Had* the man waved at him, Simon wondered. He seemed to be staring directly at him.

They lunched in a restaurant high above the harbour. A pleasant cold meal. Aunt Flo enjoyed the bread. She chattered away and as they returned to the coach, rested her hand on Simon's arm, looking at him.

'You can have no idea, dear boy, how happy you are making me. This is something I shall remember all my life. It makes such a

21

difference, travelling with someone you love.'

He smiled down at her, squeezing her hand gently. 'I'm enjoying it, too,' he lied.

The afternoon was spent at two large bulbs farms. The fields of golden daffodils, deep red tulips and blue hyacinths made a picture that caused many cameras to be used but Simon and Aunt Flo walked round, chatting.

'I think the Dutch people are wonderful,' she said again. 'I find Holland a most fascinating place.'

They watched the flamingoes with their long graceful movements as well as a fussy little mother duck with eight ducklings, and some beautiful pheasants. They went into the huge hothouses and saw more flowers. It seemed to Simon that his aunt never got tired. It amazed him. He had not realised old people were so tough.

As they walked back to the main building for tea, he said so. Aunt Flo chuckled.

'Dear boy, we have no choice. The only way to survive is to refuse to give in. The moment you collapse in your armchair and admit you can't make it, well . . .' She paused and laughed. 'You've had it.'

He found them a table and as they sat down, Aunt Flo touched his arm. 'There's a pretty girl over there, trying to attract your attention,' she said quietly, her eyes twinkling.

Startled, Simon turned his head. He saw a very attractive girl with dark hair piled high on her head, huge dark eyes and wearing what was obviously a very expensive fur coat.

'D'you know her?' Aunt Flo hissed.

'I don't . . .' Simon whispered back.

The girl smiled at him, put her finger to her mouth, shaking her head, turning to look at the big burly man by her side, who was talking to another man. Then the girl blew a quick kiss and as the big man turned to speak to her, she looked away from Simon.

He looked at his aunt. 'I've never seen the girl in my life.'

Aunt Flo chuckled. 'Dear boy, are you sure you're telling me the truth? She certainly knew you.' Aunt Flo put her head on one side, her eyes twinkling. 'Are you sure you're not leading a double life dear boy? I mean, you could be a sort of schizo . . . schizo . . .'

'Schizophrenic?'

She nodded. 'That's the word, dear boy. Maybe you're leading a double life and you don't know it . . .' she said, leaning forward, her eyes twinkling more than ever.

He laughed. 'You should have been a writer. Your imagination . . .'

She chuckled. 'It makes life more fun, doesn't it?'

Life was certainly fun for Aunt Flo, Simon thought as the day passed. They were driven through some attractive suburbs. Attractive if you like suburbs, of course, he thought, wondering how anyone could. He asked himself where he'd like to live if he was settling down. When this chance to join a group of doctors in fast-growing Hastings had come along through a friend of his aunt's, he had taken it. But was he happy there?

What was happiness, he wondered.

Later that night as they sat at their hotel he asked Aunt Flo. She had been talking all through dinner about the town. Didn't he think it wonderful how the Dutch had recovered from the war, the courage of them during the Occupation.

'You seem to know a lot about them,' he had teased as the plates of soup were put in front of them. 'This smells good.'

'I do,' Aunt Flo nodded. She looked up, her face mischievous. 'Believe it or not, dear boy, I was in love with a Dutchman before the war. I know I was nearly fifty but one can still be romantic. We were pen friends for I was lonely after you went to boarding school and so I advertised for pen friends all over the world and I got Carl. He came to see me once in 1939 and I fell in love but he didn't! Before the war began that was. I didn't see or hear from him for years but about ten years ago, I came out here and . . . and met his wife and children. He had died a year earlier but she took me all over Holland and told me about it. Didn't you love the hooks on the houses, dear boy? You should see the enormous grand pianos being hauled up for it's their only way of getting furniture in their flats because their stairs are so steep and narrow.'

After dinner they sat in the lounge and chatted. Some of their group had gone out to explore the night life of Amsterdam but Aunt Flo shook her head.

'Years ago I saw San Pauli in Hamburg and when you've seen that, you've seen everything,' she laughed. 'You go by all means, dear boy. I find strip-tease acts rather boring.'

He laughed. 'Frankly so do I.'

They had laughed. It wasn't a very large room but the chairs were comfortable. He would have thought Aunt Flo would be exhausted but on the contrary, she seemed bright and eager to talk.

It was then he asked her what happiness was.

'That dear boy, is a difficult question. I think it depends on the person concerned. I would say I am very happy now because I have your company and am enjoying myself. To my mind, happiness means . . .' She hesitated. 'I suppose it means being with someone I love.' She looked at him. 'Simon dear, I don't want to intrude but wasn't there a girl called Alicia . . .?'

He shivered. Even her name still had the power to hurt him.

'There was,' he said and added, 'for a brief while.'

Her eyes were thoughtful. 'You've never got

25

over it?'

'It hurt . . .' he said curtly and stood up. 'Look, Aunt Flo, I'll see if I can get us some drinks . . .'

'Lovely idea, dear boy. The finish to a perfect day,' she said with a smile.

He moved fast. He had trained himself not to think of Alicia. Or tried to! Even today, five years after it happened, her name could still revive those dreadful days when he loved her so and she . . . It was no good looking back, he told himself, as he got the drinks and carried them to Aunt Flo. The past was past and gone for ever.

Next day the wind was cold and the courier took them to meet a fairly old man with a big moustache and rather longish grey hair who showed them how clogs were made. Simon was sure that Aunt Flo had seen it done several times but she still watched fascinated. Frankly, Simon admitted to himself, he was rather bored. But boredom vanished to be replaced by amazement when the man, demonstrating, suddenly looked at him and lifted his hand in greeting, saying something very brief in Dutch and grinning.

Back in the coach, Simon thought of the number of times he had been greeted. He could only have a double, somewhere here in Holland. A strange feeling yet perhaps it was absurd to think like that for lots of people had 'doubles'.

26

It was even more startling in the diamond shop. Aunt Flo stood on tiptoe, leaning on people's shoulders to stare at the uncut diamonds and then their finished appearance.

'What pretty rings,' she said to Simon.

He was staring at the tall thin Dutchman who, in impeccable English, was describing the different stages a diamond went through.

Then he laughed. 'A pretty girl still says a diamond is her best friend . . .' He winked at Simon and then gestured towards him. 'As our good customer here could tell you.'

Simon didn't usually blush but his cheeks burned as everyone turned to stare at him, including Aunt Flo.

As they went back to the coach, she gazed up at him.

'I thought you'd never been here before, dear boy.'

'I haven't.' Simon strode rather fast and suddenly realised his aunt was breathless so slowed down. 'Sorry, Aunt Flo, I'm getting a bit fed up with this business. I've never been here nor bought a diamond ring in my life.'

Later they walked down the narrow side streets to shop, then waited outside the Royal Palace for their coach. A cold wind blew as a group of students demonstrated, chanting their slogans, holding big posters.

'I wonder what they're demonstrating about,' Aunt Flo said.

'Afraid I don't talk Dutch,' Simon told her.

'Maybe it's a pity,' she said.

CHAPTER THREE

Aunt Flo's favourite taxi driver was waiting for her at Gatwick. Simon saw her off.

'Dear boy,' the frail-looking woman said, kissing him warmly. 'I can't tell you how much I've enjoyed our little trip. It was so good of you.'

'I should thank you,' he said, laughing, 'I've never seen Holland before and I certainly got some shocks.'

She chuckled. 'Maybe you'd better have your head read, dear boy. You are sure you're not leading a double life?'

He laughed and kissed her. 'I'll come down and see you as soon as I can, Aunt Flo,' he promised. As he promised so often before, he realised guiltily, but this time he really would keep it.

The first thing he did when he was sitting in the train to take him to Hastings was to make a note in the tiny diary he always carried with him. It was so easy to forget . . .

The words reminded him of Cherry and suddenly he admitted why he was eager to get home. It was Cherry. He could not forget her which was unutterably absurd for he didn't even *know* her. It couldn't be love. He never

28

had believed in love at first sight. Even with Alicia . . .

He jerked his thoughts back. Better let sleeping dogs lie, he told himself. Back to Cherry, then. Why had she this fascination for him? Why was he so eager to see her?

Was it, he wondered, because she was the first girl to make it plain that she disliked him? Was it a challenge to the male in him? The old, old folk lore of cave men? Had her hostility made him want to grab her by the hair and force her to like him?

How did you make someone like you when she hated you? That was another question. Was it actually *him* she hated? Or was it simply because she hated *all* men and he was one of them? It could be if a man had hurt her badly. Why, he could remember when Alicia . . .

He got up, walking down the swaying train to get a cup of coffee. He hadn't thought about Alicia for months yet now . . .

It was pouring with rain when he reached the station so he took a taxi home along the front and to where number 37 stood, a tall white building with balconies, built over fifty years before if not more.

He paid the taxi and ran across the pavement, opening the door with his key, going into the lofty hall and suddenly standing still, staring ahead of him for Cherry was not sitting at the reception desk! Cherry had gone! There was a strange girl there!

He hung up his slightly wet overcoat, pushed his umbrella in the stand, and went forward.

The girl at the desk smiled at him, a tall girl with a cloud of dark hair, dark eyes and an amused smile.

'Hi . . .' she said. 'You must be Dr. Britten.' She held out her hand. 'I'm Anne Wallace, the new receptionist.'

'The new receptionist . . .' Simon repeated slowly, trying to realise the truth. Cherry had gone.

He pulled himself together and the next moment smiled.

'Yes, I'm Dr. Britten, Miss Wallace.'

'Oh, call me Anne, please. They all do.' She smiled at him, tilting back her head. 'I must say it's nice to see you're so young. Your partners are real squares, aren't they?'

'Are they?' His mind was working fast. Why had Cherry left? He'd only been away two days. What could have happened? He wondered if this girl would know . . .

At that moment Paul Donward opened the door. He came down the hall, his hand outstretched.

'Hi Simon. Good to see you. How did the trip go?' He was a big man, too fat for his own comfort but somehow he could not diet. His hand clasp was firm.

'Rather a scream, actually,' Simon said. 'But Aunt Flo loved every minute of it.'

Paul chuckled. 'I bet she did. And you? What did you think of the Dutch dollies? A pretty lot?'

'Dutch dollies?' Simon laughed. 'Sorry I'm a bit slow at thinking. Probably the double flight in two days. I'm not used to it.'

He had made a quick decision not to ask about Cherry. Although Paul was a good friend he had an irritating habit of picking on something to tease others and he was merciless about it. Simon had no desire to be teased about Cherry; particularly as he was not quite sure what he actually felt about her.

Paul grinned. 'Probably. Quite sure you're not in love with a Dutch girl?'

'I hope not,' the new receptionist said, chiming in, smiling at them both. 'I planned to hook him.'

They laughed. Paul shook his head.

'You haven't a hope, my dear. Simon is a bachelor of many years, and used to evading the wiles of such beauties as yourself. He likes to walk alone, it seems. Crazy, I think.' He glanced at his watch. 'I want to put through some calls and to the hospital. Look, Simon, have an early night and start tomorrow. You look really bushed.'

Simon nodded. 'I feel it,' he admitted, collecting the few letters that were for him and climbing the stairs slowly to the small but adequate flat he had on the third floor.

He went in and closed the door, looking

31

round. Mrs. Edwards, bless her, had put carnations on the table. The rooms were spotless and tidy. He went to the window and looked out at the grey rain-swept sea. Probably it was flight-tiredness, also the miserable-looking view, but he hadn't felt so depressed for years. Five years . . .

A drink was what he needed he told himself. A drink, a hot bath and Mrs. Edwards would bring him his dinner as usual then an early night. Tomorrow everything would be different and he would be himself again.

But tomorrow came and the depression was still there. The frank flirting of the new receptionist irritated Simon far more than it might usually have done. He kept finding the questions about Cherry on his tongue yet kept himself from asking them for he was not in the mood to be teased.

Luckily there was plenty of work to be done and the days passed until, about a week after he returned, he went through his dairy and noted the reminder about Aunt Flo.

He had forgotten her. Completely, he realised. How right Cherry Corfield was. He phoned Brighton and Aunt Flo was delighted.

'Dear boy, how sweet of you to think of me. Yes, I am fine. Yes, the weather is bad, dear boy, and spring is late but I expect we shall enjoy it all the more when it comes. How are you? You don't sound too well, to me.'

'I'm fine, Aunt Flo,' he said. 'I was a bit

tired when I got back. I wondered if you were?'

'I think one always is after those package tours, dear boy, but I enjoy them so much.'

'So did I,' he said. 'Let me know next time you're going on one, will you?'

'Of course, Simon dear. That would be lovely. I thought of going to Paris in the autumn. Say September, just for two or three days. I do love Paris.'

'That would be fine but I'll be seeing you before then,' Simon promised. 'I'll drive over my next free Sunday if that's okay?'

'Okay?' the quiet voice seemed to quiver. 'That would be lovely, Simon. I'll look forward to it.'

'Good . . .'

When he rang off, he opened his little diary and made a note. It was so little to give her and obviously meant so much to her. Why hadn't he thought of it before? he wondered. Somehow the days had always passed so swiftly and . . .

The phone bell rang. He moved fast, feeling absurdly hopeful it might be Cherry Corfield. Yet why should she phone him? She hated him. In any case, what excuse could she have?

It was Betsy Donward, Paul's wife.

'Simon, can you help me out of an awkward situation?' she asked.

'Of course.'

'Well, I'm having a few guests for dinner

tonight and one of them, a man, has backed out at the last moment. I know you don't like social dinner parties but could you stand in for once?'

He hesitated a moment. Once you get involved . . . ! If there was one thing he hated it was bridge evenings and dinner parties. Cocktail parties weren't so bad for you could always slip away if you were bored. But Betsy understood this and rarely asked him.

'Of course I will, Betsy. What time?'

'About seven. Thanks a lot, Simon. You've saved the situation. I found out you weren't on call tonight.'

'Very clever of you and far too subtle. What a fool I'd have looked had I said I was!' Simon laughed.

So did Betsy. 'You wouldn't lie to me, Simon—or would you? Why don't you like social life? I just can't understand you. A young good-looking eligible bachelor and you just won't meet people.'

Simon laughed. 'Maybe that's how I remain a bachelor.'

'Maybe that's why. Think of what you might be missing. There are so many nice girls around.'

'Betsy, how boring you make it sound. Who wants to marry a nice girl? Tell me, why are all women so determined to get bachelors safely wed? My Aunt Flo is just as bad. Every time she sees me she asks if I have a girl.'

'And have you?'

'Betsy, please. If I had, would I tell you?'

'Simon, you are the end. Honestly. What's wrong with marriage?'

'What's right with it?'

There was a silence before Betsy answered. Then she gave a funny little laugh. 'Lots of things. It isn't always one hundred per cent perfect but most of the time it's better than being alone. Anyhow see you at seven?'

'Of course. I'll try not to be late.'

'I know. It isn't always easy.'

He rang off and walked to the window. It was a perfect spring evening. He had about half an hour to shower and find a clean shirt. He whistled softly. Who would be the guests? The Donwards had many friends, some of them appallingly boring, others interesting. Betsy enjoyed her 'dinners' and having guests. She was a good soul, if only she wasn't such a do-gooder, always trying to help other people to find happiness. She meant well but some people preferred to be left alone.

Alone?

As the cold water spattered over him, he thought of that word. Somehow it had never struck him before that he was *alone*. Their practice was a big one. Being the only bachelor, he was willing to do most of the night calls so many of his evenings were split up. Then there was much to read, so many new methods and ideas to study. He liked his comfy flat, Mrs. Edwards' cossetting of him, and the friends he had. He need never be alone, unless, unless he wanted to. Maybe women saw it with different eyes.

The drive to the Donwards' house was not very pleasant for with summer in sight, the traffic was greater every day. The Donwards had a pleasant big timbered house. There were no cars parked in the cement-paved garage yard. Simon left his red sports car there and went to knock at the white front door.

But it was already open. Betsy came to greet him. She was a tall elegant woman with carefully-coiffured chestnut-brown hair, bright eyes and a quick smile.

'Bless you, Simon,' she said, lifting her face for him to kiss her lightly. 'I do hate odd numbers. Come in. One guest here already ...'

She led the way into the large lounge. Paul came forward to greet him and then turned.

'You have met our first guest, Simon,' he said, waving his hand towards the couch.

Simon stood still and stared. He'd never been so surprised in his life. Cherry!

'Yes,' he said coolly. 'We have met.'

'Sit down with her, Simon,' Betsy said, beginning to fuss a little as she always did when guests began to arrive. 'Paul will give you a drink. I must see how the dinner is going.' It was always a perfect dinner yet every time Betsy got worked up in case anything went wrong.

Simon sat down on the couch and looked at the red-headed girl. She looked back, her eyes cold.

'I wondered what had happened to you,' he said.

'Did you? I'm surprised you noticed I wasn't there,' she snapped.

Simon looked round. They were alone. He turned to her.

'Cherry, let's call it a truce. I know you dislike me though I don't know why but could we forget it while we're here? The Donwards are friends of mine . . .'

'And of mine,' she said quickly. Suddenly she smiled. It transformed her face and did something funny to him. It brought back the number of times he had thought of her, how he could not forget her and yet . . . She held out her hand. 'That's a bargain. It's a truce.'

He held her hand tightly and then let go. He didn't want to rush things. 'Why did you leave us?'

'Not from choice,' she told him as Paul came back and asked them what they would like to drink.

He also answered Simon's questions. 'She blacked out twice in one day. I told her she must go and rest. I also said it was absurd a girl with her qualifications doing a job like that. She's on holiday for three weeks and then she's going to teach at the College of Languages.'

Cherry nodded her head. She was smiling at Paul.

'Paul found me the job. I've known him for years . . .'

'But when you applied for the job, Paul didn't tell us . . .'

Paul laughed. 'I didn't want you to think I was biased or . . .'

'Or that I was a teacher's pet,' Cherry said.

Paul turned to the drink cabinet and Cherry looked at Simon thoughtfully. 'I went to school with their daughter and used to spend holidays with them. When . . . when . . .' She hesitated. 'When I wanted to change my job and leave London it so happened, by chance, that they were advertising for a receptionist. I saw it and . . . and . . . that's how I got here. What's the new receptionist like or . . .' She closed her mouth. She had been about to say: or *haven't you noticed.* Simon knew. So she still hated him!

'Efficient but irritating,' Simon said.

'Irritating?' Cherry lifted her eyebrows. 'She seemed rather nice and very attractive.'

'Maybe to some . . .' Simon jumped up to get the glasses and then came back. 'I'm afraid I'm not in the mood for teasing at the moment and she is.'

'What a pity . . .' Cherry began and then looked at him, her voice changing. 'What was the trip like? Did your Aunt Flo enjoy it?'

'Every moment. I must confess I was rather

38

bored but just watching her was a revelation. She's pretty wonderful for seventy-eight.'

'You know, Simon . . .' It was the first time she had called him that. He noticed and he saw, from the surprise in her eyes, that she had noticed it, too. He felt absurdly happy.

'Yes, Cherry?'

'I was going to say . . .' He watched a little colour flow in her cheeks and noticed how she was entwining her fingers as if nervous. 'Age has nothing to do with years. She's like Mrs. Chester. They'll never be old. Some of us are old at twenty-nine . . .' her voice was sad.

He looked at her sharply. 'I felt like that. Five years ago.'

She lifted her head, her eyes startled. 'You did?'

'Yes, I . . .'

Betsy Donward came sailing into the room, her pale yellow silk trousers swinging slightly. 'Everything all right, darlings? Paul has got you drinks? Oh, good, I've just got the sauce to finish. Be with you in a minute.'

The moment that might have allowed confidences was gone, Simon knew. He gave a little laugh. 'Betsy does flap so and her dinners are always a success.'

'D'you come to many of them?'

'Very rarely. I don't like getting involved in bridge and dinner parties.'

'Why did you come tonight? Did you know I'd be here?'

39

'No. I had no idea where you were, Cherry. Actually the man who was invited backed out at the last moment. I don't know why.'

She smiled. 'So you're here by chance.'

'Yes.' He looked at her and hesitated. 'I'm glad.'

'You are?' Her eyes seemed to twinkle, reminding him of Aunt Flo.

'Yes. I wanted to tell you how right you were. I mean, about being spoiled and selfish and all that. Being with Aunt Flo made me realise just how much a little sacrifice on my part meant to her. I never realised . . .'

'I was wrong, Simon. It wasn't selfishness on your part. Thoughtlessness. There's a big difference. I . . . I, too, was very thoughtless and I . . .'

The door opened and Betsy came sweeping in, with several people following her. In the consequent confusion of introductions and talk, Simon found himself sitting far from Cherry much to his annoyance. However, he consoled himself, he had made a move in the right direction. He knew where she was working, he knew she was a friend of Betsy's so he could always get her address, and maybe he could persuade Cherry to let the *truce* continue.

This put him in a good mood and he found himself talking and joking happily.

It was at dinner that he was asked about his trip to Amsterdam.

'Such a long way to go for one night,' Simon's neighbour, a tall white-haired woman with a monocle said.

She had the sort of accent he loathed.

'We saw a great deal,' Simon said, 'in a short time. My aunt enjoyed it.'

'Did *you*?' Paul asked, leaning forward, then getting up to refill the glasses with wine.

'In a way yes, and in a way no,' Simon said and there was one of those sudden silences that can occur in any party. 'I enjoyed Aunt Flo's obvious happiness but frankly people kept waving to me.'

'Waving to you?' Paul sounded surprised. 'Girls, of course?'

Simon laughed. 'Not always. I think four of them were men.'

'Four men waved to you?' Betsy said.

'And two girls.' Simon laughed. 'One was very amusing.' He described the little scenes when they were having tea. 'She was obviously with someone who would have disapproved of her knowing me, or perhaps just of me, for she put her fingers to her lips, looked at him and blew me a kiss . . .'

'And you don't know who she is?' Paul laughed. 'What a pity. Such a waste. Was she very pretty?'

'All right if you like that kind of hair style,' Simon began and stopped in time for just down the table was a young newly-married girl with a similar hair-do. He saw Cherry smiling.

Her red hair was shining in the candlelight, her leaf-green trouser suit made her skin look fairer than ever.

'But you don't *know* any of them?' Paul asked, as he sat down heavily and Betsy darted out to the kitchen.

'None of them. I've never been to Amsterdam before in my life.'

Betsy wheeled in the trolley. Duck and oranges were to follow the soup. Somehow the conversation changed and became more intimate as the guests talked to one another.

No mention was made of Simon's experience until much later when all the guests had gone except Cherry and Simon.

Paul had asked him to drive Cherry back to the flat she shared with two girls.

'If you don't mind, old man. I brought her out and I can take her back . . .' Paul, sprawled on the couch, legs stretched out, said.

'Be a pleasure . . .' Simon said and smiled at Cherry, 'If Cherry doesn't mind.'

'What choice have I?' she teased and he knew another moment of glee. She had said it in such a friendly way. The truce must surely be lasting?

'I've been thinking, Simon,' Paul went on, after the last guest had vanished and the four of them were sitting talking, having a final drink. 'You must have a double in Amsterdam.'

Simon laughed. 'That's what I think. Aunt

42

Flo suggested I was a schizophrenic and led a double life.'

'Do you?' Cherry asked with a sweet smile.

'I hardly think so.' He laughed. 'I'd have noticed the stamps on my passport, I guess.' He turned to Paul. 'A double sounds most likely. I suppose most of us have doubles.'

'Yes, but you must be very alike, Simon. I could understand one person mistaking you for another but . . . was it six?'

'Something like that. The man at the diamond place made a strange remark as Aunt Flo noticed. He said diamonds were a girl's best friend as, and then looked at me and added; 'as our good customer here could tell you.' It was most embarrassing. Everyone stared at me. One or two made jokes and poor Aunt Flo was really puzzled.'

'So . . .' Paul said, making a little steeple of his hands as he folded them in front of him. 'Your double is a sort of Don Juan, as the girl couldn't venture to admit knowing him yet blew him a kiss, also he must be wealthy as he's obviously bought more than one diamond ring. What were the others like who knew you?'

'Well, there was the man who showed us how to make the clogs. He gave me a real . . . how shall I say, meaningful grin, and said something in Dutch. Another man looked at Aunt Flo and then at me and said something about I was having a bit of a change, I imagine

43

he meant that Aunt Flo was rather older than my usual companions . . . Well . . . I suppose this sort of thing happens to us all at sometime or other.'

Paul sat up. 'Well, I think you should do something constructive about it.'

'Constructive?' Simon began to laugh. 'What could I do about it that was constructive?'

'Trace your double and find out who he is,' Paul said.

'But why? What's the point?'

Simon was laughing but Paul's face was grave.

'Just that it could be awkward for you, Simon. Doctors are, as you know vulnerable.'

'You mean it?' Simon asked, then looked at them all.

Betsy nodded. 'A danger recognised is a danger halved . . .' she said seriously.

Simon began to laugh. 'You're kidding me . . .'

Cherry looked at him. 'I think they're right, Simon. It could be embarrassing for you. I mean these . . . these cases in which identification can be made wrongly could apply here, couldn't it? If he did some crime and you were accused . . .'

'What shall I do, then?' Simon was still amused.

'Go over to Amsterdam and trace him,' Paul said.

Simon spread out his hands and shrugged.

'What good would that do? Am I to tell him to behave himself, in case I am accused of his wrongdoings?' He laughed 'In any case, I can't speak Dutch.

Cherry leaned forward. 'But I can.'

There was a sudden silence. Simon stared at her, amazed, finding it impossible to believe what he had heard.

'You mean you'd come with me?'

She smiled. 'Why not? On a strictly business proposition, of course. I shall expect my expenses paid plus wages. I'm rather broke at the moment so it will come in handy.'

Betsy clapped her hands. 'It sounds super. Cherry is so good at languages, Simon, and . . .'

Paul joined in. 'The change will do Cherry good, too. She needs a complete rest and this might prove rather amusing. You'll probably have a queue of girls waiting to tell you that they love you, Simon . . .' He exploded with laughter. 'Gee. I wish I could be there . . .'

Cherry stood up. 'I really think we should be going. Betsy must be tired out after cooking that gorgeous dinner. I wish you'd let me help you wash up, Betsy.'

'No trouble at all. I just put it in my washing-up machine and in the morning my Mrs. Mops comes to give me a hand. When will you go, Simon?'

Paul stood up. 'I'll fix it with the others tomorrow, Simon. No one will mind. You do far more than your share of night work. I'll

45

look forward to hearing what you find out . . .'

Standing by the car in the still warm spring evening, Simon looked at his host. 'Your trouble, Paul, is too much imagination,' he said. 'I doubt if I'll find anyone that's like me and if I do, then what?'

'At least you'll know he exists.'

'What difference does it make?'

Paul laughed. 'I don't know . . . We'll talk about it tomorrow.'

With Cherry by his side, Simon drove back to Hastings.

'Whereabouts do you live?' he asked.

'I share a flat with a girl at the Green. D'you know where it is?'

'Yes. Nice district. Will you like your new job?'

'Teaching? Oh yes. That's what I was doing in London.'

'I see.' Carefully he changed the subject. Some man must have hurt her badly and she could not bear to think of it. Just as he had felt about Alicia. That was odd, he hadn't thought of her for several days. Maybe he was getting over it.

He left her at the Green. 'Thanks for offering to come with me to Holland.'

'I shall benefit. I've always wanted to see the bulbs and they should be even better now than when you were there,' Cherry said, her voice cool again.

'Cherry.' Standing by her side, Simon caught

her hand. 'Look, promise me one thing. The truce continues until we come back from Amsterdam. Promise?'

She looked at him thoughtfully and then smiled.

'I promise. Goodnight and thanks for the lift. You'll let me know when we're going? I'm free all the time. Now . . .' she added, her voice sad as it had been once before.

Simon drove home, singing quietly. Things were working out his way. The trip to Amsterdam and the search together, while ridiculous, could help to make them know one another better. Perhaps the truce would go on and peace be made? Once he found out why she hated men—and he, in particular— perhaps things would change.

Next day he and Paul had a talk alone. 'Actually, Simon, I agree with you. There is no point in the search nor can you do anything. We all have doubles and they do little or no harm. The truth is, old man, that I did it to help Cherry. It seemed the absolute answer.'

'Help Cherry?' Simon accepted the cigarette Paul offered him, and drew out his lighter. 'Does she need help?'

'And how. You must be blind if you don't see it.'

'I gather she hates men and so I guessed that something had happened.'

'I'll say. The rotten swine.' Good-tempered Paul rarely sounded so angry.

'He walked out on her. Just a few weeks before the wedding. No letter, no reason, he just vanished. She had something of a breakdown at the time and then went back to work but I gather it hurt too much, for everyone knew and she hates pity. She's an independent girl and I knew that if she thought *we* were helping *her*, she'd turn it down. I know she's hard-up at the moment, that she needs a change of air and scene and when you talked of this double, well, frankly, old man, it seemed the answer.'

Simon stared at him. 'I think you're right. Well, I'll see she has a good time.'

'Tactfully, Simon. She's as edgy as a . . . a hedgehog.'

Simon laughed. 'Don't I know it,' he said ruefully.

CHAPTER FOUR

Simon found the flight from Gatwick disappointing. He was not sure what he had expected but the result was certainly not what he had hoped for.

They travelled by car and parked at Gatwick, hurried inside to get everything smoothed out, and ended up at the wrong deck. Luckily they saw the mistake in time and hurried back along the long glass-windowed corridors but unfortunately, or at least so it was to Simon, by the time they got on the plane it was nearly full.

This meant they sat far apart and it was not until they were walking in the cold wind at Amsterdam that Simon had a chance to speak to Cherry.

'Everything okay?' he asked.

As he looked down at her, he silently blessed Paul Donward for having given him this opportunity to get to know Cherry better. She was wearing a green macintosh over white slacks and shirt and she had a green scarf tied round her red hair. 'Of course,' she said coolly. 'Why shouldn't it have?'

'I just wondered,' he said lamely. 'Some people don't like flying.'

'I'm not crazy about it but one has to accept it these days. Trains are so slow and irritating. Where are we staying?'

'I've got the address here . . .' Simon searched his pockets without success. 'I'm sure I put it . . .'

'Have you looked in the pocket of your overnight case?' Cherry asked quietly.

He smiled. 'I didn't think of that. Thanks.' He found the papers he wanted and looked at them. 'Can we get a taxi? I mean most of these people seem to be going by coach.'

'Most of them are package tours. We can get a taxi over here . . .' She led the way. He followed her. There was no doubt she was most efficient. Her knowledge of Dutch, too, would help.

Help what? he asked himself. After all, this was really rather a farce. What did it matter if he did have a double here in Amsterdam? Lots of people were mistaken for others. Of course, as Paul had said, it was a perfect chance to take Cherry's mind off her recent misery and give her a short holiday.

Poor girl, Simon thought as she spoke to the taxi driver. How it hurt to be jilted. He knew! Never would he forget the pain; the humiliating guilt-ridden hurt that he still felt after five years. Looking back, he could remember the hours he spent going over their conversations, their frequent quarrels. Had it been his fault Alicia stopped loving him? Or had she never loved him at all and had it just been a game for her? Sometimes he wondered if it wouldn't be easier to bear the death of someone you loved. True, it must be horribly final but at least you knew he, or she had loved you. Being jilted made you doubt that. Then there was the knowledge that perhaps she now loved someone else . . .

'Get in, Simon,' Cherry said impatiently. 'What were you thinking about?'

'You,' he wanted to say but decided it might be unwise. So he smiled: 'Me . . .' he told her, which was part truth.

The hotel seemed quite nice. He had a pleasant single room overlooking the Dam.

50

Cherry was on the floor above.

They had lunch in a restaurant that was high up above the town. Cherry got down to business when they were having coffee. She pulled out a notebook and pencil.

'I want you to tell me just who the people were who seemed to know you,' she said crisply.

Simon folded his arms, half closed his eyes, as he thought back. Then he mentioned the man who had been hurrying to catch a plane.

'He said, "Bit of a change, man" looking at Aunt Flo, and then added "Be seeing you".'

'Can you remember what he was like, Simon?'

'Ye-es. A big man with a red moustache. Yes and dark glasses. I remember noticing them for it was a cold windy day and no sun. I wondered if he had eye trouble . . .'

Cherry bent over her notebook, her pencil flying.

'The next?'

Simon frowned. 'A man on a bicycle. Waved and shouted the same thing: "Be seeing you".'

'Which shows that your double must be living here and not on a visit,' Cherry said thoughtfully, chewing the pencil. 'I mean, if you . . . I mean *he* had only been here off and on, they wouldn't say so casually: "Be seeing you" would they?'

Simon had been intently watching the way her face changed as she spoke, and her eyes lit

51

up, and then the sudden gravity that made her look prettier than ever.

'What . . . er? Oh yes, I quite agree.'

Cherry looked up, her pencil poised. 'Simon, if you want me to help you, you must co-operate.'

'I'm sorry. My thoughts were miles away.'

'Obviously. Now who else . . .?'

Simon thought for a moment and said: 'The man who showed us how clogs were made. He said something in Dutch and smiled at me. Obviously he knew me well. I mean, there was a sort of . . . of knowledge in his smile, if you know what I mean.'

'I think I do,' Cherry's voice was cool. 'Obviously he was accustomed to seeing you with pretty girls.'

'Not me . . . my double,' Simon said quickly.

She nodded and chewed the pencil again. 'What was he like? D'you remember where he was? I mean, I think we should go and see him, don't you?'

'Well, he wasn't very young. He had a big grey moustache and his hair needed cutting. He seemed a humorous sort of chap and enjoyed talking to us all. Where it was . . .? I'm not sure I can tell you that. The names of the streets are so unpronounceable I can't remember them.'

'D'you ever remember anything?' Cherry asked, but her voice was teasing rather than sarcastic.

Simon smiled. 'I rang Aunt Flo before I left.'

Cherry nodded. 'Bully for you. She must have been surprised.'

Simon's cheeks felt hot. 'Actually she was. She was also delighted to hear I was coming over here again. She has a thing about Holland.'

'Lots of people have. Now where were we? Oh, yes, when did you go and see him? Was it the day you arrived?'

'No, the morning after.'

Cherry nodded thoughtfully. 'I can probably find out from the travelling agencies. They'll know which clogmaker your package tour visited. And the diamond man? That seems to me even more important. What exactly did he say?'

Briefly Simon told her about the day diamond cutting was explained and how they watched the diamonds being polished.

'Then we saw the rings.'

'And what did the man say? Would you know him again?'

'I think so. He said something about pretty girls liking diamonds and then said their good customer should know and he looked pointedly at me. I mean, it was quite definitely me he was referring to.'

'I see.' Cherry closed her notebook with a snap and put it and the pencil in her large crocodile handbag. 'Let's get moving.'

'Right away? Couldn't we just see the bulbs today and flop?' Simon asked. 'We can investigate tomorrow.'

Cherry looked disapproving. 'I think, Dr. Britten, you have forgotten we are here for a purpose and not for fun.'

He shrugged. 'As you say . . .'

He waited in the hall while Cherry phoned.

He was impressed by the excellent English he heard all round him. Remembering what the girl courier had said when she told them that at Dutch schools they *had* to learn French, German and English, he found himself wishing that English schools had such a doctrine. How much easier it was to travel when you were a good linguist. He never had been good at languages, or maybe he was too lazy, but the French he remembered had something to do with his Aunt's pen at the bottom of the garden. He had asked the courier why the languages were a *must* and she had given him the most sensible answer he'd ever heard.

'This is a small country with a language used nowhere else. So if we are to do business or have jobs as secretaries or couriers or anything like that, we must be able to talk the other languages.'

That made sense. The English were notoriously lazy where languages were concerned and he was one of the worst of them.

Cherry joined him and nodded. 'Fine. I

managed to get the addresses of both. Come along. We'll have to have a taxi to the clog-making shop . . .'

There was a large group of people crowding round the man who was explaining and demonstrating how those wooden shoes, known throughout the world as Dutch symbols, as well, of course, as having a practical use, were made. Simon and Cherry kept in the background but as the crowd went out through the door and before another group arrived, Cherry took Simon forward and spoke to the man who had a big grey moustache.

The man smiled welcomingly. 'Ah, Mr. Britten . . .' he said and then spoke in Dutch. He paused, looking puzzled, when Simon made no answer

'Mjnheer . . .' Cherry said and burst into a long speech in Dutch. Simon stood by her side, feeling rather a fool, until she turned to him. 'He says he has been giving you Dutch lessons as you hope to marry a wealthy Dutch girl and felt you should talk Dutch . . .' she said.

Simon looked startled. 'Me? Marry a Dutch girl?'

The man smiled. His English was good. 'But that what you said, Mr. Britten. She is very beautiful as well as rich. Often you bring her to see me.'

'But I've never been here before. Oh yes, about ten days ago with my Aunt . . .'

'I remember.' The man smiled again. 'A charming but delicate old lady who hardly took her eyes from your face. I see that you charm them of every age.'

Simon's cheeks burned but the man went on:

'You have, however, been here several times since that day. I give you lessons in Dutch. You slow learner.' He smiled.

'Mjnheer,' Cherry said politely. 'You call this gentleman *Mr.* Britten but he isn't, you know. This is Dr. Britten and he lives in England.'

The man looked puzzled. 'That cannot be. You told me Australia.'

'Australia?' Simon echoed. 'But I've never been there.'

Cherry spoke quickly: 'Mjnheer, we think Dr. Britten has a double here in Amsterdam. He is always being mistaken for someone else . . .'

The man's face crinkled with amusement. 'Ah . . . that must be most amusing. Perhaps I should say embarrassing. Dr. Britten would, perhaps, be well advised to return to England where he is known as himself.'

'Who is this man . . .' Cherry began but at that moment, a crowd of tourists came surging in, to surround the equipment that was used to demonstrate the making of clogs.

She caught hold of Simon's arm. 'Let's get out of here,' she said quietly and, after some effort, they managed to weave their way out

56

into the crisp spring sunshine.

'Whew . . .' Simon whistled. 'Then I *have* got a double.'

Cherry gave him a strange look. 'Unless you're leading a double life.' She looked at her watch. 'We'd better get back to town before the diamond shop is closed. I told the taxi to wait . . .'

Back in Amsterdam with the tall houses standing close together as if packed in sardine tins, and the fascinating gables that Aunt Flo had loved, as well as the small statues and engravings that decorated so many of the houses, Simon felt a bit exasperated. If only Cherry didn't take it all so seriously. How could he give her the holiday Paul said she needed if they were going to rush from one place to another?

They went into the diamond cutters and joined a group of tourists who watched the demonstrator as he explained how an ordinary looking bit of heavy glass became a valuable sparkling diamond.

'Is it the same man?' Cherry hissed as they looked at the rings that were finally displayed.

'No.'

Cherry hovered and as the group moved away, she smiled at the well-dressed man who had been talking to them all.

'Could I have another look at the rings? There was such a crowd.'

'But of course,' he said with a smile,

bringing the tray out. He looked at Simon, his mouth twisted wryly. 'It is pleasant to see you again, Mr. Britten. We are always delighted.'

Simon spoke before Cherry did. 'I am Dr. Britten and I have never bought a ring here.'

The man looked puzzled. 'But you are one of our best customers, Mr. Britten.' He looked at Cherry and then back at Simon and shrugged. 'Ah, is it that I have been indiscreet? If so, I make the apologies.'

Cherry looked up with a smile. 'No, I'm only his temporary secretary. We're trying to trace a man who looks like Dr. Britten . . .'

'*Doctor* Britten? I was not aware . . .'

Simon sighed. 'Look, it isn't really important but I came over here about ten days ago for the first time. Several people seemed to know me and I wondered if I had a double . . .'

The man was trying not to smile. 'This is a new line, Mr. Britten. Most amusing.'

Feeling his temper was running out, Simon turned to Cherry. 'Let's forget it, now, Cherry. At least, I do know I have a double here . . .'

'Just a moment . . .' She turned back to the man. 'Could you find the name Mr. Britten uses? I mean Christian name.'

He bowed. 'But certainly. I will be only a moment.' He hurried off, leaving the tray of rings on the counter.

'Why d'you want to know that?' Simon asked, irritably.

58

Cherry frowned. 'Can't you see? I want to know if he is deliberately pretending to be you. If he is, he'll be signing himself Simon Britten, won't he?'

The man returned. 'No Christian name. Simply S. Britten on his cheques.'

'Thank you,' Cherry hesitated. 'Could you tell us something about him?' She saw the frown on his face and added hastily. 'No. It's all right . . .'

'All I know,' the man said stiffly, ' is that Mr. Britten is a good customer, that he has been in Amsterdam for several months, that he came from Australia and is shortly marrying one of Holland's wealthiest girls. He is popular but also has enemies. Does that satisfy you?'

Cherry nodded. 'Thank you. Thank you very much.'

Once they were back at the hotel, they went to their rooms, showered and changed. Cherry met Simon down in the hotel lounge and he leapt to his feet, his eyes widening as he stared at her. She was wearing a white dress with a high waistline. It came down to her ankles with gold ribbon round the neck and in her short curly red hair nestled white camellias.

'You're quite an eyeful . . .' he said admiringly.

She smiled and did a little curtsy. 'Thank you, kind sir. You did say something about going out to dinner and dancing.'

'Yes, I did.' Simon smiled. He'd said it but

59

with little hope of it coming true. 'Shall we have a drink here first?'

'That would be lovely and we could go over what we've learned.'

'Must we?' Simon asked. 'Couldn't we forget it for one night?'

She frowned. 'Simon Britten, I think you're forgetting that we're here for a purpose not just to enjoy ourselves. We haven't much time as we're going back tomorrow so we mustn't waste it.'

He sighed. 'All right.'

The drinks came and Cherry talked. 'First we know your double is an Australian, that his Christian name begins with S. We also know he has an eye for the girls and is engaged to a very wealthy one. He seems to be popular but obviously annoys some people. It must be a strange kind of annoyance to make enemies of them. Maybe he steals their girls. He seems to have quite a name . . . Simon, I've been thinking. Perhaps we should get a private detective to help us.'

Simon stared in horror. 'But why?'

'Well, you want to know about him, don't you?'

'In a way but . . . It's just one of those coincidences that happen but no one will believe. Look . . .' He drained his glass and stood up. 'Let's go and enjoy ourselves tonight. We'll decide in the morning. Okay?'

She followed his example, putting down her

empty glass and standing up. 'Okay.'

The restaurant he took her to was lavish, the last word in extravagant luxury, the lights pleasantly low, an excellent band. The dinner was venison followed by a strange fruit dish that was intriguingly tasty. Afterwards they danced.

Cherry was a beautiful dancer, he thought, as he held her lightly in his arms. He rested his chin on top of her red hair and wondered if he'd made any progress yet. Did she still hate him because he was a man, of the gender she loathed because one had hurt her so much. Was it still only a truce between them? A truce that might be ended when this trip was over?

They were just walking back to their table when suddenly, from another table, a girl came towards them.

She was tall, taller than Cherry. Her hair was blonde and piled high on her head. She was beautiful but her eyes were blazing with anger as she moved swiftly, her long old-gold dress swinging as she walked.

'So this is where you are . . .' she said to Simon. 'You could have phoned, written or something. How d'you think I felt? Walking out on me like that. My parents are furious . . .'

Simon stared at her in something like dismay. 'Excuse me, I don't know you. I'm . . .'

'A liar and a cheat . . .' she almost shouted the words, her hand flying and with a loud clap, hitting his cheek.

Simon took a step back, his hand going to the red mark.

'I . . .'

Cherry grabbed his arm. 'Let's get out of here . . .' she said and hustled him through the tables to the reception hall. 'Wait here for me . . .' she said and before he could stop her, she was gone.

It seemed an interminable age before she returned. She looked pale and even rather exhausted.

'What happened?'

'Just a hammer and tongs row. She refused to believe you weren't your double. She said *she* ought to know you if anyone did for you're the man she was going to marry . . . There were one or two very hostile men with her that's why I got you out of the way. They just won't believe that you're not the Shawn Britten they know.'

'Shawn . . . is that his name?'

'Apparently. Let's go back to the hotel, Simon. Our evening is spoilt.'

'I haven't paid . . .'

'I have. You can pay me back later. I've got a migraine. I'd like to go back to the hotel . . .'

'Of course,' he said and asked the commissionaire at the door to call a taxi.

They sat in it silently. At the hotel, Cherry said goodnight and went to her room. Simon sat for a long time in the bar, slowly turning an empty glass round and round. So much for his carefully planned chatting-up of Cherry! She had been quite strange, almost as if she no longer believed him either. Who on earth could this double of his be?

Over breakfast they discussed the situation. Simon was all for giving up. He was startled when Cherry sighed and agreed.

'What made you change your mind?' he asked her.

She looked at him, her fingers crumbling the crisp roll on her plate. 'Simon, would it be possible for you to be Shawn Britten without knowing it?'

He stared at her. 'You must be joking?'

She sighed. 'No, I'm not. They're all so sure you're that other man.'

'Now look, Cherry, let's be practical,' he said rather crossly. 'How could I, a hard working doctor, find time to slip over here and be the sort of Don Juan this man obviously is. If I was a schizophrenic. I wouldn't be able to do it without giving the show away. How about passports? No, it doesn't make sense.'

She pushed the plate in front of her. 'None of it makes sense, Simon. When does our flight go?'

'Two-thirty.'

'Could we do some shopping first? I'd like to get my mother a present and something for my young cousins.'

'Okay,' he said and knew he sounded sulky. But he felt it. Most decidedly he did. The trip had not been the success he hoped. If anything, it had made her trust him less.

That morning, knowing he was acting badly but feeling in a sullen mood, Simon followed Cherry round the shops, down the narrow side streets, waiting with silent patience as she chose a brooch for her mother, fashioned like a heart with a small blue stone in the centre, and some tiny Dutch dolls for her cousins. They ended up in the big square with the modern War Memorial and the Royal Palace.

Perhaps Cherry was aware of his unnatural silence for she kept talking of superficial things, the Royal Palace, for example, almost as if his silence disturbed her.

'It was originally the Town Hall, here, and then made a Royal Palace but they only use it for ceremonial occasions. The Queen doesn't live in it. Oh, look at those pigeons? Come and see them . . .'

She took his arm and led him across the road to the square where hundreds of pigeons were being fed by tourists.

'Reminds me of Trafalgar Square . . .' Cherry went on.

Suddenly they heard the beating of a drum, the blaring of a trumpet, and the chanting of Dutch words.

'Oh no . . .' Cherry said. 'A demonstration. We'd better get out of here.'

'There was one when we were here before. What are they demonstrating about . . .' Simon began but it seemed as if the people around them had also decided to move for there was a sudden surge and everyone seemed to be pushing each other across the road and down the side streets. Simon could see the students marching, waving big placards as they chanted words he could not understand.

He looked round for Cherry but she had vanished. He pushed his way through the groups, now standing on the pavements, watching the students as they gathered in the square.

'Where was Cherry?' he asked himself. She couldn't just vanish. Unless she was annoyed with him for his silence and had seized the opportunity to go back to the hotel alone.

He managed to get out of the crowd by going down a narrow road. He looked up at the Dutch name and wondered how it was pronounced. The best thing to do was to find the hotel and wait there for her. They'd left their luggage there, meaning to collect it later before going to the Airport.

It was easier said than done, for he went down one narrow side street after another, going in a circle and finding himself back at the Square. It was back to normal again, the demonstrators had moved on. But there was no sign of Cherry.

He tried to remember how they had reached the Square in the first place and after what seemed hours, he eventually reached the hotel. He went up to his room, gathered his small overnight case and various things he left around and prepared to go downstairs, to wait in the hall. He could probably get a drink while waiting.

There was an impatient knock on his door. He went and opened it. Cherry stood there, her hair rumpled, her face flushed and her eyes angry.

'How could you be so mean . . .' she began.

'Hey, steady on,' Simon said. 'What's this about? Where did you vanish?'

'What's it about . . .!' she came, almost storming, into the room. 'What sort of man are you? Standing there, laughing and talking to that girl, and there was I . . . there was . . . was I . . .'

Simon closed the door, took Cherry by the arm and made her sit down. 'Look, stop being hysterical,' he said sharply and added: 'When you've calmed down. you can tell me what I did that was so mean.'

She sat still for a moment, glaring at him. Then fumbled in her handbag for a tissue and blew her nose. Finally she took a long breath and looked up.

'How could you have stood there when you saw those men annoying me.'

Simon frowned. 'I stood there while the men annoyed you?'

'Yes, you did. You looked at me and never showed a sign, never smiled or said anything.

66

You just laughed and talked to the girl and . . . and I had an awful job with the men. Oh, they weren't nasty. They just wanted to pick me up . . . You could have come over . . .'

Simon moved fast to her side, grabbing her shoulders, shaking her. 'Snap out of it. Are you accusing me of letting you be chatted up by two men?'

'*I . . . I . . .*'

'I'm fed up to the teeth with this nonsense,' Simon roared. Never had he felt so angry. 'I did not see you in the crowd. You suddenly vanished and I looked everywhere for you. I decided you were mad at me for being moody and had come back here. I tried to find the darn place and it took hours. Finally I saw a road called Lidesi . . . something or other.'

'Leidseplein . . .?' she asked.

'That's it. Finally I got to the Square and came back here.'

'Then . . . then it wasn't you?'

'It most certainly was not me. And thank you for the compliment you've paid me. You think I am the type of man who is out with a girl and can let two strangers chat her up while I laugh with another girl. Thank you very much . . . thank you very much indeed. It just shows what a high opinion you have of me . . .' he said furiously and walked to the door.

'I'm going to get a drink. I need one. We shall be leaving in half an hour. Please be ready.'

He even slammed the door as he went away. He was shaking with fury. Not so much with Cherry for her foolishness in not trusting him but with his double for making such a mess of a weekend that might have been a start of something more than just a friendship ...

He'd had three brandies when Cherry joined him. She was pale. 'Simon,' she said very quietly. 'I'm sorry. I'm very sorry. It's just that I can't trust anyone at the moment. Not even you.'

Simon took hold of her hands. They were cold and, for a moment, her fingers clung to his. 'That's all right, Cherry. Sorry I lost my temper.'

'I don't blame you. Simon, I'm worried ...' She sat down by his side, frowning a little. 'You see, it could be quite dangerous for you. If he fooled even *me* ...'

Simon laughed. 'Look, have a quick drink and then we'll go. I think the sooner we're off Amsterdam soil the better.'

'I am sorry. Simon, really I am but ...'

He smiled at her. 'Don't worry, Cherry,' he said gently. 'I can understand.'

CHAPTER FIVE

Paul was eager to hear the result of the brief trip. The night after Simon and Cherry got home, he invited Simon for drinks at the local club.

'We can talk better when the females are not around,' Paul said with a laugh. 'How did it go? Did Cherry confide in you? I hoped she would. Get it off her chest. As it is, all her misery is bottled up inside her.'

Simon relaxed in the deep leather armchair. 'Well, no she didn't actually confide,' he admitted. 'But on the way home, she talked. She did say she hated all men because one man had let her down. She also told me how she and her mother had been so close and then when her mother married again, everything went wrong.'

'Yes, I gather the step-father was jealous.'

'I gathered that, too, but Cherry blames herself. She said she and her mother had always been so close that she never thought to be any different and that she should have known better. Cherry blames herself for everything . . .' Simon said, remembering what had been in many ways the best part of the brief trip, which was the flight home from Amsterdam.

They had gone on the plane early so had sat together and somehow got talking.

'She blames herself for love failure, too,' Simon went on. 'Says she thinks she loved him too much and got possessive. I wish she'd stop blaming herself for everything. She told me she knew she was a failure . . .'

'Cherry?' Paul gave a half-grunt, half-laugh. 'She must be daft. That girl is the most efficient, intelligent girl I know, as well as one of the prettiest. How can she be a failure?'

Simon offered Paul a cigarette then lighted one for himself as well. 'That's what I said and she just stared at me. "But can't you see," she said, "it's emotionally that I'm such a flop. I can do practical things, like learning languages, playing chess but when it comes to loving I'm a flop."'

'What did you say?' Paul asked, his eyes thoughtful.

'What could I say? I told her that few relationships with a step-father are successful. That he was as much to blame as she was. As for the man she loved, I told her he was a heel and she was well rid of him. I also told her that I knew that made no difference and that she must stop blaming all men for what one man did.' Simon gave a little laugh. 'I'm a fine one to talk. D'you know, Paul, five years ago a girl broke my heart. It's still cracked. So I have a good idea how that poor girl feels.'

'I wondered why you showed so little interest in the female sex,' Paul said, his eyes amused. 'Surely, man, it's time you grew up? Clinging to past memories isn't healthy, you know.'

'I know but can you give me the recipe of how to forget them?'

Paul waved his hands vaguely. 'Touché.

70

Well, now we've talked about Cherry and I'm sure it'll have done her good to weep on your sympathetic shoulder, Simon but what about your double. Was there one?'

'And how!' Simon said bitterly and proceeded to tell Paul all that had happened.

Of course the part about the girl smacking Simon's face in front of the crowd in the restaurant made Paul rock with laughter but when Simon said how Cherry had believed she'd seen him, Paul's face grew grave.

'I see what Cherry means. If *she* was fooled . . . You know, Simon, it's a good thing your double is in Amsterdam, it could make things dicey for you.'

'I don't know,' Simon said, stubbing out his cigarette, 'Frankly I'm a bit fed-up with the whole thing. What I can't make out is the coincidence that he has my name. My surname, anyhow, and oddly enough his Christian name is Shawn, also an S. I mean, Paul, it seems to me too much of a good thing. Looking like me and with the same name.'

Paul tapped his fingers on the side of the chair and frowned thoughtfully. 'You were an only child?'

'Yes—and my father was an only child. My mother had a sister, just the one, and she is Aunt Flo who's never married.'

'So that cuts out the chance of him being a cousin. Why should anyone deliberately make himself look like you and build up a reputation

'. . .' Paul stopped. 'I don't get it. I just don't . . .'

'Neither do I. Let's forget it,' Simon said. 'I'd better be on my way. Time I got back or Mrs. Edwards will start flapping.'

He went back to his flat and for the first time, felt alone. After he had eaten, he hesitated and then rang Cherry's phone number.

A strange girl answered him. 'Cherry? I'm afraid she's asleep. Who's calling? Can I give her a message? Oh, Dr. Britten.' Her voice changed. 'I'll tell her.'

'Thanks. I just phoned to hear how her migraine was.'

'Pretty bad,' the unknown girl said. 'That's why I sent her to bed early.'

'A good idea. By the way, who's her doctor?'

'Dr. Donward, I think.'

'I just wondered. Only I think she should see him if the migraine doesn't go.'

'It won't,' the girl said, 'Until she falls out of love with that . . . that . . .' She paused. 'Know what I mean?'

'Yes, I do. Well just tell her I called. She'll be starting work soon. Maybe that'll help.'

The unknown girl gave a funny hooting laugh. 'Nothing'll help. I know that.' And she slammed down the receiver.

Slowly Simon replaced his. How right she was. Nothing can help. Not even time.

He went to the window. Their belated spring was proving beautiful. The sea looked so calm, the sky cloudlessly blue. He half-closed his eyes and for a moment saw Alicia vividly, with her laughing face, her blue eyes, that golden hair, her hands that moved so fast as she talked, her husky voice.

If he couldn't get over Alicia, how could he expect Cherry to forget her love? Yet, in many ways, he *was* getting over Alicia. Since Cherry entered his life, he had thought less often of Alicia. Maybe in time he'd forget her altogether. Was that the recipe for recovery? To fall in love with someone else?

Perhaps one day Cherry . . .

But the days passed and every attempt he made to get to know Cherry better seemed doomed for failure. When he rang her, she was invariably either out or in her bath, only once did he manage to get her and asked her out to dinner but she said, 'Thank you but I'd rather not if you don't mind', and slammed down the receiver!

He stood still for a long time, staring at the phone. Now what had that meant? She'd rather not? Was she still unsure whether he was the man in Amsterdam? Had their brief friendship still left her unable to trust him? Surely just going out to dinner? What was she scared of? Getting involved again? But perhaps the secret of regaining happiness was to get involved?

One perfect Sunday he drove over to Brighton, noticing how the trees were all in

73

leaf, the blackthorn white on the hedges, the trees flowering, Aunt Flo, however, was not too well. He had not warned her he was coming and she was surprised as well as delighted, but he looked worriedly at the frail little figure in the armchair, near the open window that led to a small balcony overlooking the sea.

'What's wrong, Aunt Flo?'

'*Anno domini*, dear boy,' Aunt Flo said with a little smile.

'You've seen your doctor?'

'Of course. I'm not that foolish, Simon. He gave me some pills and said I must rest. So I am.' She smiled at him. 'This is a lovely surprise, dear boy. Please don't worry about me. One often has these ups and downs and when it is warmer, I'll be a new woman.'

'Who is looking after you?' Simon asked, glancing round the small room anxiously. It all seemed clean and cared for.

'A very dear girl who has the flat above me. She'll be down later and will make us a cup of coffee. You'll stay for lunch, of course.'

'I was going to take you out.'

She smiled. 'Not today, dear boy. Some other time. Now do tell me what happened when you went to Amsterdam. Did you go alone?'

'Well, no, not exactly. I took a secretary with me. A temporary,' he added, hastily, telling her about Cherry. 'Actually Paul Donward

74

wanted me to get her away even for a day or two. She was let down by a man she loved and . . . well, she can't get over it.'

'Is she a nice girl? Isn't she the one you told me about?'

Simon nodded and smiled. 'But don't get big ideas, Aunt Flo. She has no time for me. I've asked her out to dinner but she's not interested.'

'She must either be blind or very silly.'

He laughed. 'Not everyone thinks as highly of me as you do.'

'Well, they ought to. Now what happened? I'm longing to hear.' Her pale cheeks were flushed, her eyes bright as she leaned forward. 'Do go on, dear boy.'

He told her about the flight, the visit to the clog man, to the diamond shop.

'The extraordinary thing is,' he went on, 'that this double of mine has the same . . .'

The door opened and a girl of about twenty looked in.

'Aunt Flo—ready for your cup of coffee?'

'Oh, Teresa dear, do come in and meet my dear nephew. Simon, this is my neighbour. So very kind . . .'

The girl came into the room. She wore blue jeans and a rather crumpled pink blouse, her dark hair was in rollers and she blushed. 'I didn't know your nephew was coming. I must look a sight.'

Simon had stood up. He smiled. 'A pleasant

75

sight, if I may say so. You must be absolutely smashing when dolled up.'

She laughed. 'I work all the week so have to do my house-work when I can.'

'Simon, d'you know she comes back every lunch time to look after me. I don't know what I'd do without her.'

Teresa blushed. 'I'm happy to. You see . . . you see . . .' she looked at Simon. 'I lost my mother a few months ago and it helps to have . . . have someone like Aunt Flo. I'll make us some coffee.' She disappeared into the tiny kitchen.

'Such a sweet girl,' Aunt Flo said. 'So kind.'

'I can see that,' Simon sat down.

'Do go on. You saw the clog man and the diamond man and they both thought you were someone else and then what happened?'

Simon told her about the embarrassing scene at the restaurant. Aunt Flo didn't laugh, as Paul had. She looked distressed.

'Poor boy. How awful you must have felt. What a sensible quick thinker this Cherry girl seems.'

'She's most efficient and seems to enjoy it.'

'So you went back to the hotel?'

'Next day we went shopping . . .' Simon told about the demonstrators, losing Cherry, and her fury when she found him. 'You know she really thought it was me. That frightened her. She said that if even she couldn't know the difference . . .'

76

Aunt Flo's eyes brightened. 'She said that? If even she . . . ?'

'Yes, she seemed worried for she said she'd have sworn it was me. She said that just showed in an identification . . .'

The door opened and Teresa wheeled in a small trolley.

'You're a doctor?' she said as she sat down and poured out the coffee.

'And a very good one,' Aunt Flo said.

Teresa's eyes twinkled. 'So I gather. Your aunt never stops talking about you.'

It was a pleasant day. Teresa cooked the lunch and shared it with them. Then vanished for the afternoon, returning to make the tea. When Simon went she walked down the stairs and out on to the front where his car was parked.

'I'm most grateful,' Simon began.

Teresa looked at him. 'Don't be. I'm the one who should be grateful. I think I'd have gone mad if I hadn't Aunt Flo. I know she needs someone and . . . and . . .' She bit her lower lip and looked away. 'I miss Mum so much. I don't know what I've have done if I hadn't Aunt Flo.'

He ran his finger along the door of his car. 'You know, she ought to go somewhere . . .' he paused. 'Somewhere where she can be looked after.'

'I'm looking after her,' Teresa said quickly.

'But you can't all the time and if you have to

work . . .'

'If she gets worse I'll stop working. I . . . I don't *have* to work. Mum left me enough money. Dad died years ago and . . . well, we're not wealthy but I can manage.' She looked up at him earnestly. 'Please, please, Simon, don't put her in an old ladies' home. It would kill her.'

'I know. Teresa, will you let me pay you a salary?' He saw her quick response and stopped her. 'Please. Aunt Flo has done so much for me and I've done so little for her. If I knew she had you . . . She's proud, too, you know and . . .'

'Yes, she is. All right.' She smiled. 'I might be able to get a wheelchair. Then I could take her out. She hates being shut in. She loves people.'

'Yes,' he said and added silently: and so do you!

He drove back to his flat. It was quiet. So very quiet.

Spring departed and suddenly summer came. The front was more crowded now—with wheelchairs and old people gallantly walking in the sun, and children playing on the beach while the dogs raced round, barking excitedly.

One perfect day Simon woke. A usual day, promising to be busy, the sun shining. He had his usual surgery and afterwards went up to his flat where a delicious cold chicken and salad was waiting.

'Mrs. Edwards, what would I do without you?' Simon asked as the tall, slightly-bent, grey-haired woman brought him coffee.

She smiled. 'You'd fend for yourself all right. We women like to think men can't do without us but they can. I've known ever so many widowers who've coped and enjoyed it.'

He laughed. 'You don't think then that we really need you?'

She lifted a finger. 'I won't generalise but you obviously don't need anything but a housekeeper.'

'What makes you say that?'

'Well . . .' she laughed. 'If you needed a woman for anything but cooking your meals, ironing your shirts, making your beds and being generally useful, wouldn't you have got wed years ago?' She stacked the plates on the tray. 'I've three sons. Each one different. Jake married at twenty-two, Peter is still a bachelor at thirty, and Frank at twenty-six has . . . well, he falls in and out of love all the time. Maybe he'll settle down one day but he's in no hurry.'

She left the room. In no hurry . . . he thought slowly. He was in no hurry to make Cherry love him? Put it a different way, he thought. He didn't want to hurry her for people could be caught on the rebound and that was not a good idea. One thing, he'd completely forgotten Alicia. Hadn't thought of her for weeks. But Cherry . . . Why did she deliberately avoid him?

On impulse, he phoned Betsy Donward.

'Simon?' Betsy sounded startled. 'This is unusual.'

'I want your help.'

'You do?' Her voice changed, became wary. 'In what way?'

'Betsy, I know you won't jump to conclusions like Paul does but I'd like a chance to get to know Cherry Corfield better.'

'Oh Cherry? Oh . . .' Betsy began to laugh. 'You like her?'

'Very much but I'd like to know her better, Betsy. Every time I ask her out, she digs up some feeble excuse. What does a man do then?'

Betsy laughed. There was relief in it and momentarily, he wondered why. 'Easily arranged. Ring the wife of your best friend and she'll ask the two of you for dinner. Right?'

'Right,' he said 'You're an angel.'

'Simon . . .' the tone of her voice changed again. 'You weren't here yesterday?'

'No, my day off.'

'What did you do?'

Simon was surprised for Betsy Donward was not an inquisitive type. 'I went for a drive. Lovely day and I felt I wanted to get away,' he said.

Which was not the complete truth. He had seen the sun shining and suddenly thought of Aunt Flo in her small room with that narrow balcony. How she would enjoy a trip out in the car, he had thought, and had immediately driven over to Brighton only to find the flat empty. Much later, after worryingly visiting the hospital and after some trouble, he had found the caretaker who had no idea what had happened.

'That young lady what lives in the flat above, she's bought a car. Maybe she's taken your aunt for a drive. She often does. Take her out, I mean.'

He had no idea how long they would be out or where they had gone so Simon had driven inland, driving aimlessly, feeling ashamed because he had not thought of going over before on his days off. How easy it was to be selfish.

Now he heard Betsy sigh. 'You just went for a drive. I see. Okay, Simon. I'll fix something with Cherry.'

'Thanks,' he said, hanging up the receiver, looking at his watch. Time to start on his rounds. He wondered if Betsy would tell Cherry it had been his idea. No. Betsy was more diplomatic than that. He felt suddenly happy going out to his car.

He saw two small boys sitting on the pavement edge, reading a newspaper. He recognised them as sons of one of his patients. They turned to look at him and began to giggle.

'What's the joke?' Simon asked but with one of them clutching the newspaper, they went racing off, laughing like crazy kids.

Simon shrugged, looking at his list. Old Mrs. Chester was his first patient.

She was sitting on a wooden box outside her front door in the sunshine. Simon walked up the narrow cobbled path that led to her small house and she waved to him.

'I'll have none of that nonsense about me going back to hospital, young man,' she shouted.

Simon squatted by her side. Offered her a cigarette which she took, then lit it for her, and lighted one for himself. 'Dr. Donward is a bit worried about you.'

'Dr. Donward is a twit,' she said and roared with laughter.

Simon looked at her thoughtfully. 'He seems to think you'd do what *I* said.'

'He did?' her voice raised at once.

Simon laughed. 'I told him he was mad. That you were an ornery old hedgehog, liable to stick out your prickles at a moment's notice.'

She frowned. 'Am I as bad as that?'

Simon grinned. 'That was the under-statement of the year.'

She patted her white hair. 'I hate hospitals.'

'Don't we all. Unfortunately we can't always choose.'

'Look, what do they want to do to me? I'm scared. Happen once they get me in, they won't let me go.'

Laughing, Simon tried to explain. 'Look, Mrs. Chester. Hospital beds are hard to get. I promise you they won't keep you in a day, or an hour, longer than necessary. I give you my word . . .'

Her tired old eyes narrowed. 'Cross your heart and hope to die?'

He performed the childish motions. 'I do, indeed,' he promised.

'But what's wrong with me? Happen I am always tired, happen my nose keeps bleeding and a rare mess it makes, too . . .' She chuckled. 'Frightens my neighbours to death, it does. Can you stop that, young man?'

Simon looked at her gravely. 'I'll make no promises, Mrs. Chester,' he said slowly. 'But I think we can.'

She smiled. 'I like your way of talking. Okay, then, I give in.'

He stood up. 'I'm glad. I'll make arrangements for an ambulance to fetch you, Mrs. Chester.'

She caught hold of his hand. 'You'll come and see me? I feel . . . well sorta safe if you're around.'

He smiled. 'That's a nice compliment. Of course I'll be around . . .'

'That reminds me . . .' she said, 'In the paper this morning . . .'

'I'm terribly sorry, Mrs. Chester. There's nothing I'd like more than to stay and have a chat, but I've a long list so if you'll excuse me . . .'

It wasn't until he was in the car that he remembered something Cherry had said. That he had been thoughtless and selfish for these old people might have no one else to talk to all day. Surely he could have spared her another ten minutes?

He started the engine and drove to his next patient. A small boy with a broken leg whose mother had to work and who was cared for, somewhat vaguely, by a neighbour. Of course, Simon told himself, as he drove up the steep street, if he gave an extra ten minutes to every lonely patient . . . Well, time just wouldn't allow it.

Back at the end of a long busy afternoon, he was greeted by Anne Wallace, the receptionist who had, by now, given up any attempt to 'chat him.' She gave him a strange look.

'Read the papers today, Doctor?' she asked.

He shook his head, sorting out the letters on her desk.

'Hadn't time.'

'Hmm . . .' she said thoughtfully. He looked up, and saw her eyes bright with curiosity. She turned away. 'You've got a visitor. Mrs. Edwards let her into your flat.'

'A visitor?'

He went up the stairs quickly. Was it Betsy? Yet surely she would phone?

He opened the front door and stood, amazed. There was a girl standing by the window, gazing out at the sunny sea. She turned round.

'Cherry . . .' he said delightedly and wondered if she had noticed his immediate reaction.

She didn't smile. 'Simon,' she asked. 'Where were you yesterday?'

'Yesterday? I drove over to Brighton to see Aunt Flo . . .' He was puzzled. 'What made you . . .'

'Oh, good . . .' Cherry sank into a chair as if exhausted. 'You've got a witness?'

Simon went across the room to stand by her. 'What is all this?' he asked, frowning. 'Look, that's the second time today I've been asked that question.'

'Did you see the morning papers?'

'No, I didn't. I had to rush out and . . .'

'I think, perhaps, you'd better see them,' she said, picking a newspaper up from the floor and spreading it out. 'Look . . .' she pointed to a drawing

He stared at it. It was a sketch, drawn by a method know as identikit.

'But . . .' he began and then stopped. The identikit could be himself.

'You see what I mean?' Cherry said, standing close to him. 'It looks just like you. But then so did your double in Amsterdam.'

Simon was really startled. 'You mean, you think . . .'

'Read it,' she ordered.

He picked up the paper. It was a short

description of a bank hold-up. A man had pushed a note across to a teller, demanding money, threatening he would drop the shopping basket he carried and a bomb would explode. As the teller began to collect the money, the man pushed another note under the protective screen, picked up the basket and walked out of the bank. The second note was an apology, saying it was a hoax. The teller had immediately sent for the police but by then, the man had gone. However, the bank had been full and a number of people had noticed the man who was wanted now for questioning, hence the identikit.

'I don't get it . . .' he said slowly.

Cherry shook her head. 'Simon, please wake up. That's your double . . . unless it was you . . .'

He put down the paper and looked at her. 'D'you think it was? D'you honestly think I'd do such a damfool dangerous thing? If one of the customers had had a dicey heart . . .'

'That's what I thought at once. I knew you wouldn't play a joke like that. That's why I've been waiting to see you, Simon. The police may come for you. They are looking for this man. Have you a good alibi? If not, I'll say you were with me.'

Simon put his hands on her shoulders. 'You'd lie for me?'

She looked up at him steadily. 'Of course.'

He had never felt so happy in his life. She would lie for him. That meant . . . He bent to kiss her and the phone bell shrilled. Cherry moved away, her hand pressed against her mouth.

'That's the police,' she said scared.

Simon laughed. 'Nonsense.'

But it was the police. He listened, said Certainly. Of course, he quite understood and replaced the receiver slowly. He turned to look at Cherry.

'They would like to ask me some questions,' he began to laugh. 'It's all so ridiculous.'

'But Simon, is it? I would have sworn in Amsterdam that it was you I saw with that girl. These people will swear you were in the bank. Where were you? You did see Aunt Flo?'

'No, she was out. But I did see the caretaker.'

'What time?'

He frowned. 'I can't remember exactly. It was mid-afternoon. I went in the morning and she wasn't there so I went up to the hospital— I thought she might be ill, and then had lunch and then went back, in case she'd returned. Then after a lot of trouble, I found the caretaker.'

'This . . . this stupid joke happened in the morning. You could have been in London.'

'But I wasn't. Look, I said I'd go down right away.'

'Can I come with you?' Cherry caught hold of his arm.

He looked down at her. 'Of course but . . .'

'I'll wait outside in the car.'

'Fine,' he said.

Inwardly he was delighted for Fate was playing into his hands. How . . . how wonderful that she wanted to help him. It just showed . . . What did it show?

He warned himself to go slow, not to hope too much. Maybe she would be like this to anyone in trouble. For obviously she thought he was in real trouble.

He drove to the police station and went inside. In a surprisingly short time he rejoined her, looking a bit rueful.

'I'm not sure they believe me.' He sat by her side, swinging round to face her.

'You told them about your double?'

He nodded. 'They said it was a likely story . . . I said it was the truth. They took down Aunt Flo's address and the caretaker will be interviewed and I am not to leave the district.' He laughed.

Cherry's hand curled round his arm, 'Simon, you can joke but I think we should treat it more seriously. You're quite sure you have no relations that could look like you?'

'Quite sure.'

'Look, Simon, what do they mean *leave the district*?'

'Well, I suppose that I must go on living here. Why?'

'I wondered if we could go and see your Aunt Flo. I think it's too much of a coincidence that this man who looks like you could have the same name. Either he must be a relation or it is someone deliberately trying to injure you.' She sighed as he grinned. 'Your trouble, Simon, is that you're too nice a person.'

'I am?' He was startled.

'Yes. You trust people, you see only good in people but Simon, you know, life isn't like that. You might have an enemy who is jealous of you or wants to hurt you. This hoax might be part of his plan. I mean, it isn't very good publicity for a doctor is it?'

'I've had no publicity.'

'But you will. I bet your name'll be in all the papers tomorrow. Who told the police your name? Or didn't they tell you?'

'Oh yes, they said several patients of mine rang up.'

'Swine,' Cherry said.

Simon began to laugh. 'You really are taking this seriously. It's darned nice of you, Cherry but . . .'

'Will you do me a favour, Simon?' Cherry said sharply, her eyes thoughtful.

'Of course.'

'Drive me to Brighton. I'd like to meet your Aunt Flo.'

'Now? I ought to ring her and . . .'

'We can at the first public phone box we see. The police won't mind? They'll probably follow you.'

Simon started the engine. 'Honestly, Cherry, you must have been watching T.V. too much. I'm sure they won't.'

At the first visible public phone box, at Warrior Square actually, Simon made two calls. One to the receptionist to say he would not be back until late that evening. He was not on call so it didn't matter. Then he rang Aunt Flo.

'Could I drop in tonight to see you?' he asked.

'Of course, dear boy. How absolutely lovely.'

'D'you mind if I bring a friend?'

'Simon, is it Cherry?' Aunt Flo asked, her voice excited.

'Yes. If you don't mind?'

'Mind? I'm delighted. You'll stay for supper?'

'You don't want us for that. I thought we'd dine on the way. It's a chance . . .'

Aunt Flo chuckled. 'Diabolically clever, you young men. Of course, candles and soft music and then you come on to visit me. At least we can have a drink. I shall look forward to it.'

'Fine.'

Cherry was looking thoughtful as he joined her. She was wearing a thin blue linen coat, matching trousers and a white blouse. Her red hair was blown about by the wind but it was naturally curly. She looked up. 'Okay?'

'She's delighted.' He slid in the seat by her

90

side. 'I said we'd have dinner first . . .'

'But . . .'

'She invited us to dinner and I had to think of some excuse. She will do too much and she'd probably flap like mad and produce some elaborate dish.'

Cherry smiled. 'I see. Very thoughtful of you.'

'She's been longing to meet you.'

'She's heard about me?' Cherry sounded surprised.

'Of course. She knows you went with me to Amsterdam.'

'You have told her about the double?'

'Of course,' Simon said as he drove along the Front and past the Sun Lounge and the huge ship-like block of flats.

'Did you tell her his name was yours?'

'I . . . I'm not sure. I remember we were talking about him and then Teresa . . .'

'Teresa?'

'She's the girl in the flat above Aunt Flo. She's very good and does a lot for the old girl. I'm going to pay her a salary for she's given up her work to nurse Aunt Flo.'

'Why?'

Simon shrugged. 'I think she needs someone to love. She recently lost her mother and said it helped her having someone to look after.'

'I can understand . . .' Cherry looked away from him. 'It does.'

CHAPTER SIX

Simon enjoyed the early part of the evening. They found a nice restaurant, had a pleasant meal, talking more easily than ever before but Cherry still looked worried and when they got into the car again and were driving along the coastal road, she looked out to sea and sighed.

'I do hope Aunt Flo can help us.'

Us, Simon thought happily. She couldn't really hate him and be worried about him. He began to whistle.

Cherry turned to him. 'I can't understand how you can keep so calm. Your whole career, perhaps . . . perhaps you'll be sent to prison and . . .'

'They've got to prove I did it.'

'You've got to prove you didn't.'

Simon parked the car outside the big block of flats and led the way. He rang the bell on Aunt Flo's door which was almost immediately opened by Teresa.

She smiled a welcome, her eyes running quickly over Cherry. This time Teresa had had warning and was wearing a pretty pink and white voile frock, her hair a mass of curls.

'Come in,' she said warmly. 'Aunt Flo is thrilled.'

Aunt Flo was. She struggled to her feet, frail little figure that she was, her arms open wide to embrace her nephew and then she beamed at Cherry.

'How lovely to see you both. Do sit down. Please choose the most comfortable chair. Teresa will get us a cup of coffee and later we will have drinks.'

Cherry obeyed, sitting on the couch while Simon chose a deep rather aged armchair. Looking round quickly, Cherry saw that the flat was crowded with antiques, ornaments and pictures. How hard it must be, Cherry thought, to part with memories for that is what these things meant to old people.

The coffee came in and Teresa hovered round as Simon and Cherry talked casually with Aunt Flo, waiting for the right moment to start asking questions. Cherry began it.

'Did you see this morning's paper, Aunt Flo?'

The old lady beamed. 'No, dear, but Teresa read it to me. I've broken my glasses and I can't see.'

Cherry looked quickly at Teresa who nodded slowly, her eyes saying what her mouth did not. Cherry smiled and began to like Teresa.

'Well, Aunt Flo, you know we told you about Simon's double . . .' she began.

The front door bell shrilled. Aunt Flo looked startled. 'Now who could that be? At this hour? See that the chain is across before you open the door, Teresa, my dear. I don't want you bashed . . .'

Teresa laughed and left the room. She gave a funny little cry and Simon jumped up but before he could reach the door, it had opened and a man stood there.

Simon found he was staring at himself.

The man stared back. Aunt Flo caught her breath, her hand across her heart. Only Cherry remained calm though she was surprised. She saw Teresa in the doorway, looking absolutely shocked.

Then the second Simon spoke. He stepped forward, holding out his hand.

'Hi, brother Simon . . .' he said and grinned. 'So we've met up at last.'

'Who . . . who are you?' Aunt Flo asked, her voice breathless.

He saw her as if he hadn't noticed her before. 'You must be Aunt Flo,' he said, going to her side. 'The solicitors told me about you and gave me your address. Mr. O'Shea is dead, of course.'

'Of course but . . .' Then her face changed as she understood. 'You're Shawn?'

He nodded. 'Yes, the other twin . . .'

'Other twin . . .' Simon stepped towards them. 'Look, your name is Shawn Britten and you say you are my twin brother? But my mother only had one child and she died when I was born . . .'

Aunt Flo lifted a wrinkled hand. 'There were twins, dear boy,' she said. 'I never told

94

you as I was afraid you would be terribly hurt and jealous because your father had taken Shawn with him to Australia. You were the delicate baby and Shawn the healthy one so, you see, maybe I should have told you, but I was afraid you'd feel . . . well, rejected by your own father.' She looked up at the tall man and smiled. 'It is good to see you, Shawn, after all these years. Sit down and make yourself at home. Sit down all of you, this is a moment for rejoicing.'

*   *   *

Simon sprawled in a chair. Shawn sat by Cherry's side on the couch. Teresa hovered in the background, her eyes going from one man to another.

Aunt Flo saw her and laughed. 'Teresa, dear, don't look so dazed. They are twins that's all.'

'But they're so terribly alike.'

'Not in behaviour,' Cherry said.

Shawn turned to look at her, his eyes twinkling in amusement. 'Am I the baddie?'

She looked straight at him. 'Aren't you? Have you seen today's papers?'

A slight flush tinged his cheeks. 'Yes, I was a fool, wasn't I. I knew at the time but . . .'

Simon leant forward. 'It was you?'

'Who else?'

'Who was him and what?' Aunt Flo said

95

eagerly.

Shawn turned to her now, he shrugged. 'I was a fool, Aunt Flo. A stupid fool. I'll tell you what happened. Where shall I start? At the very beginning or about . . . about the newspaper drawing.'

'The newspaper,' Cherry said before anyone else could speak. 'You owe Simon an apology. He's already been questioned by the police.'

'He has?' Shawn looked horrified. 'I say. I am . . .'

'The police? What have they to do with it?' Aunt Flo asked. 'Did you have a car crash, Simon dear boy?'

'It wasn't Simon, Aunt Flo.' Cherry said quickly. 'It was . . . it was Shawn.'

Shawn sighed. 'Okay I'll tell you that bit first. I got to England day before yesterday. Went along to the solicitors to get Simon's address then went to a little pub off the Strand. Whom should I meet but a crowd of Aussies, old pals of mine. They . . . well, let's face it, we had a party. They baited me. I always fell for that sort of thing. You see, believe it or not, I am very English. My father was, my step-mother . . .' He saw Aunt Flo's questioning eyes. 'Yes, Dad married soon after we got to Australia. I'll tell you all about that, later, Aunt Flo. Anyhow, we were very English and proud of it. These pals of mine began ranting about degenerate England, how it was going to the dogs, and then they ran down the

96

police force. Now I was brought up to believe that an English cop sets an example to the world so I stood up for them. Then they suggested we prove it. That we did a bank hold-up to see how quick the police reacted. I refused to do it. Then they put our names in a hat and said they'd draw the man. Of course my name was drawn. I didn't look but I wouldn't mind betting each of my pals wrote my name down . . .' He laughed. 'Anyhow . . . I finally agreed. But I'd got the second note printed, too. I think it was when I saw the look on the teller's face that I realised the enormity of what I was doing.'

'Had it been an older man, he might have died instantly of a heart attack,' Cherry said coldly.

'I know. Perhaps that was why I chose the young man. Anyhow I pushed the note through and walked out. It was no longer funny.'

'It certainly wasn't.' Cherry's eyes flashed furiously. 'And now Simon is involved and a doctor doesn't . . .'

'How is Simon involved?' Aunt Flo's frail voice asked.

Cherry turned to her. 'The identikit drawing was in the newspaper. Some of Simon's patients kindly rang the police. They questioned Simon tonight and he isn't allowed to leave the town. That's why I made him come here. I was beginning to think there was something fishy about this man who was getting Simon involved . . .'

'On the contrary,' Shawn said. 'Simon got me involved.'

Simon rubbed his cheek. 'It was you she thought she was hitting . . .'

Shawn laughed. 'I couldn't make out why she apologised . . .'

'Please . . . please . . .' Aunt Flo was laughing. 'I'm lost. Teresa, would you bring in the drinks and let's straighten this out. You, Shawn, played a stupid trick but you didn't mean to hurt Simon?'

'Of course not. It never occurred to me . . .' Shawn paused, looking at Cherry. 'You don't believe me, do you?'

She stared at him. 'I'm trying to.'

He smiled. 'Thanks. Half the battle's won.' He turned back to Aunt Flo. 'Maybe I'd better start at the beginning.'

She smiled back. 'Shawn, it is so nice to have you here. Please start right from when you got to Australia.'

'I will. Not that I can remember much . . .' He laughed. 'I was only a small child. I remember Dad telling me how good they were on the ship, the stewardess looking after me. Maybe she was after him. He was quite good-looking . . .'

'It's funny,' Simon said slowly. 'I've never thought of my father in all these years. What was he like?'

'I'll tell you,' Shawn said, his voice hard.

He told them how, soon after they reached Australia, his father re-married. 'My step-mother didn't like having a child around during those first years, I don't think. Not that she was cruel but she was never my mother. Not like Aunt Flo . . .' Shawn said, looking at Simon.

'How did you know? I mean, how do you know?' Cherry asked.

Shawn turned to her. 'This comes out later, if you don't mind. Anyhow I went to school and Dad was nearly always away from home. An engineer. Did very well, too. He wanted me to follow in his footsteps but it left me cold. I wanted to be an architect. I'm afraid Dad was disappointed in me . . .'

'Me, too,' Simon said quietly.

Shawn looked at him. 'But that was Dad. I said just now I'd tell you about him. Maybe Aunt Flo will back me up but she's such a loyal old soul. I doubt it.' He smiled at the old lady. 'My father . . . I should say, our father, Simon, was the most selfish . . . well, ladies present so I won't say the word. He only thought of himself. He wanted to be proud of me and wasn't. He made my step-mother unhappy and the two girls were scared stiff of his temper. When he came home life was grim.'

He looked at them all. 'Maybe I shouldn't say such things about Dad but they're true. He thought only of himself. He left everything to

99

me. Not a penny to his second wife.'

'All to you?' Cherry chimed in. 'But . . .'

Shawn grinned. '*But* is right. Don't worry. I saw to that. He left a good sum. I saw that my step-mother is okay and so are the kids. I came over to give his share to Simon . . .'

Simon had been leaning forward, arms stretched between his legs as he clenched and unclenched his hands. Oddly enough, it hurt him to hear his father spoken of in this way.

But now he looked up. 'Me? But why . . .'

'Because you're entitled to it. You're his son. Look, let's go back to the telling of the whole thing. I was an architect and I lived not far from home. My own flat, of course.' He grinned at Teresa and Cherry. 'Plenty of pretty girls. I've an eye for them.'

'I know,' Cherry said coldly. 'I saw that in Amsterdam.'

'Of course.' Shawn clicked his fingers. 'You were the pretty girl who kept smiling at me . . .'

'Smiling at you,' Cherry nearly exploded. 'I thought you were Simon and I was mad as . . . mad as anything for the two men were trying to pick me up and I thought Simon would rescue me and . . .'

'I'm not surprised you really thought he was Simon,' Aunt Flo said. 'They are very alike. Do go on, Shawn dear boy.'

'Where was I? Oh yes. I did quite well. Saw Dad fairly often. There was a . . . call it a façade of affection but I knew darned well he

100

had no time for me. Anyhow I bought myself a new car. A Jaguar.' He gave a harsh little laugh. 'Was I proud of it. How childish can you be. I remember Dad making some nasty remark about the luck of single men who aren't hampered by women clinging with babies round them. I saw my step-mother close her eyes. He was always hitting at her. Making out it was her fault they had two daughters. He'd wanted another son. One he could be proud of. I'm afraid,' Shawn hesitated, looking at Simon. 'You and I let him down. Anyhow, I asked Dad if he'd like to come for a ride in the car. I thought it might lighten the atmosphere in the house which was pretty tense. So we went ...'

He paused, folded his arms, closed his eyes and sighed.

'Don't worry. I know all the answers. I've had 'em and they don't help one bit. I killed my father. Not intentionally, of course. In fact it wasn't my fault. This huge trailer ... we were behind it on a hill. Dad kept telling me to pass it but I wasn't happy. A bit of a blind rise higher up and cars race down there. The trailer was so long I'd not have had a hope to get past it ... Anyhow, the trailer broke away. I don't know why. They found it was a rotten rusted chain or something. Anyhow it came back into us ... we went back into the car behind and so an ...' He sighed. 'A nasty sight, I was told. I knew nothing. Woke up days later

101

in hospital with two broken legs, three ribs cracked and concussion. Dad was killed. Outright.'

'But that wasn't your fault,' Cherry said quickly.

Shawn looked at her. 'No but if I hadn't asked him out . . .'

'And if he hadn't been nasty to your step-mother . . .'

Shawn smiled ruefully. 'I know. I've been told all that. It still hurts, though.'

'It wasn't your fault, dear boy,' Aunt Flo said gently. 'You must have been very ill.'

'I took a long time recovering. Some tripe about psychotic damage or something . . . So . . . well. I went through Dad's papers. He always hoarded things. Actually my step-mother didn't want me to. She said an odd thing: Let sleeping dogs lie. I think she knew I was going to divide the money and she wanted your share, Simon, for her kids. Anyhow I got tough and insisted on going through Dad's papers. I had nothing much to do in hospital. Normally I doubt if I would have and if I hadn't, then I would never have known I had a twin brother.'

'Your father didn't tell you?' Aunt Flo asked.

'No. He told my step-mother, though. She knew. But I didn't.' Shawn looked at Aunt Flo. 'Dad had kept your letters. They were all opened, so I imagine he read them.'

'He never answered once, Shawn.'

'He was a lousy letter writer. Gee,' Shawn turned to Simon. 'You don't know how lucky you were having someone like Aunt Flo to look after you. Those letters of hers, she describes you so proudly. And the snaps of you.' Shawn shook his head slowly. 'I wish I'd been the kid that was left behind.'

Aunt Flo dabbed her eyes with her lace edged hankie. 'I'd have loved you both. I always wished your father had left you, too, Shawn.'

'So do I . . .' he said and smiled at her.

Cherry caught her breath. It was Simon's smile. It was absurd how alike the two men were. To look at, of course.

Teresa moved quietly round the room, refilling the glasses. Cherry turned hers slowly round and round.

'And then?' she said. 'You read your father's papers, found you'd been left the lot and that you had a twin brother. What did you do?'

'After I'd fixed things with my solicitor I travelled by ship . . .'

'And met a pretty girl,' Cherry said with a strange smile. 'The girl who slapped Simon's face. Because of your behaviour.'

Shawn laughed. He looked at Simon and shook his head slowly. 'I'm sure sorry about that, Simon. It was unintentional. Yes, I came by ship and fell in love with Madeleine Zykmayer. You must admit she is very beautiful. Well, we got pretty serious and she

103

asked me to visit her parents so I thought, well, I haven't seen my brother for years, a few more months won't matter, so I stayed in Amsterdam . . .'

'And learned Dutch from the clog-maker,' Cherry said. Some of the disapproval in her voice had vanished.

Shawn smiled. 'You certainly did your private-eye stuff well. Yes. I had a really good time . . . and then . . . and then . . .' His face clouded for a moment: 'Well, honestly I wasn't well. I went to the doctor and he frightened me.' Shawn grinned at Simon. 'Seemed like what was wrong might be serious so he took certain tests. I didn't tell Madeleine or anyone. I just vanished for the tests. Came back for a few days but kept out of Madeleine's way as I didn't want her asking awkward questions. My fault, of course. I wasn't staying with her parents. I was working and had my own flat. Madeleine and I had actually been quarrelling. She was very possessive and wanted to boss me around.' He grinned. 'I don't know if you're the same, Simon, but I do hate bossy women. Anyhow I got the result of the tests and the whole thing was okay. The doctor was wrong and I was all right. I was in a fine mood, rushing off to see Madeleine and she apologised for smacking my face.'

He chuckled as he looked at them. 'Then I knew that by some strange unbelievable coincidence my twin brother must be around.

After all, Madeleine said she would have sworn it was me.'

'I said that about you being Simon,' Cherry admitted.

'Well. I went around and a few people told me things about you. That you were asking questions and that you were a doctor so I knew it was you. I would have come over at once but . . .' He laughed ruefully. 'Another car crash. I wasn't driving this time. Poor Madeleine was. She's out of hospital now though we were both in for a while. I'm still not a hundred per cent.'

'Are you going to marry her?' Cherry asked bluntly.

Shawn grinned. 'Maybe. Maybe not. We fight all the time and then make up. I think, perhaps, I'm getting a little tired of her, though. She will plan everything ahead, not asking but telling me, if you know what I mean.' He looked at Cherry, his eyes twinkling. 'Of course, you are not like that.'

Cherry's cheeks grew hot. 'Maybe I am.' She looked at Simon. 'Am I, Simon?'

He smiled. 'Not often and then only when it's good for me.'

They all laughed. Shawn stretched out his legs, looking at his watch. 'I'll get a train back to London and go straight to the police.' He saw their surprised looks. 'Well, I must, mustn't I? Can't have Simon thrown into jail for what his twin brother did. The least I can do.'

'Actually it's too late,' Cherry said, her voice cold again. 'You've damaged his name irre . . . irre . . .'

Shawn grinned. 'Irreparably. Hadn't heard that word in years. I know I must have . . .' He became serious. 'I had no intention of involving Simon. I'll tell the police and it'll be in all the papers . . .'

'But people will still say there's never smoke without fire and . . .' Cherry began.

Simon leant forward. 'What's done is done, Cherry. Shawn didn't mean to injure my reputation and I'm sure my real friends will understand. Those that don't aren't worth worrying about.'

'I agree,' Teresa said quickly. 'Simon is quite right.'

Cherry looked up as if startled and then looked at Aunt Flo.

She was nodding. 'Live and let live, Cherry dear. It was a foolish thing for Shawn to do but all young men do foolish things, especially after a party. He's said he's sorry and that is enough.'

Cherry went red. 'You're right, of course. I'm sorry, Shawn.' She hesitated. 'Wouldn't it be better if you came with us and went to the local police station with Simon?' she asked. 'You see, he told them about you. I mean, about the double for he didn't know it was you, of course, and they called him a liar.'

Simon laughed. 'Not quite, Cherry. Let's say

they implied it.'

'What's the difference? They owe you an apology,' Cherry said firmly.

Shawn nodded. 'Could be she's right, Simon. Will I be able to get a train back to town as late as we'll be?'

'Why not stay with me?' Simon asked. 'I can lend you a toothbrush.'

Shawn grinned. 'Nothing I'd like better.'

They all stood up, bending down in turn to kiss the suddenly quiet old lady. She pressed Shawn's hand.

'Welcome home, dear boy. I hope to see you again.'

'You will. You most certainly will,' he promised.

After they had gone, Aunt Flo looked at Teresa.

'Well?' she asked.

'Well what?' Teresa asked with a laugh, tidying up after the visitors.

'Well, he is handsome, don't you think?'

Teresa lifted an eyebrow and smiled. 'I think they both are. I'm not sure which one I like best.'

'You know, dear girl, you've got something there,' Aunt Flo said softly and waited until Teresa had left the room before she added: 'Poor Cherry.'

CHAPTER SEVEN

Cherry sat in front of the car, wedged between two men, as Simon drove home. He spoke little but Cherry and Shawn never seemed to stop talking.

'Tell me about Australia,' she said with that eager note Simon loved to hear in her voice.

Once Shawn started, he seemed he would never stop. Simon concentrated on the driving though occasionally he heard Shawn's lavish descriptions of the wonderful beaches and the water ski-ing and the winter months when they went up into the Snowy Mountains.

'We have everything . . .' Shawn said proudly.

He told them how most of the houses were single storeyed. 'I loathe climbing stairs,' he admitted with a laugh. 'Bone lazy, that's me.'

And Cherry laughed too. 'Then I'll never invite you round to meet my friends because we're on the fifth floor and there's no lift.'

'Fifth floor . . .' Shawn whistled. 'No wonder you're so slim.'

He told them about yachting, about the harbour at Sydney and the fabulous bridge and the crazy Opera House.

'Any man out there can make a fortune provided he's willing to work.'

'And of course,' Cherry chimed in. 'it's such

a democratic country there's no snobbery.'

Shawn hesitated before answering. 'Well, yes and no. We do have snobs but for a different reason. Our measure is money. It doesn't matter who your Dad was so long as you've got the lolly. In fact, it even goes further than that for a girl can't find a good husband—by that I mean materially, of course—unless she goes to the right school.'

'I'd never have thought . . .' Cherry sounded shocked.

Shawn laughed. 'Oh no one's perfect in this world. The point is, Cherry, that Australians respect the people who *make* money. It has nothing to do with birth, which is something that is no credit to you because you had no say in the matter. But if you become a tycoon or a millionaire that's due to your work so you're respected.'

'That's one way of putting it,' Simon said dryly. 'It isn't everyone wants to make a fortune or the best workers who get paid the most.'

'I agree with you, any road,' Shawn said.

Cherry laughed almost excitedly. 'Shawn, that's north country words. *Any road* . . .'

'Is it?' Shawn sounded surprised. 'Maybe because my step-mother was North country and kids pick up phrases now and then.'

They reached St. Leonards at last. Simon spoke curtly without turning.

'We'll drop you off first, Cherry.'

'Oh but . . .' she began, looking up at him.

He shook his head. 'I don't know how long we'll be at the police station.'

'Of course. I forgot.' She sounded sad. 'Shawn, I do hope it won't be too awful. What d'you think'll happen?'

'I haven't a clue. What say you, Simon?'

Simon shrugged. 'I should imagine a fine and a warning. After all it's your first offence. It *is* your first?' he added. 'Only they'll probably contact Australia.'

'Of course it's his first and it wasn't really an offence,' Cherry said indignantly. 'It was just a stupid childish . . .'

Shawn laughed. 'You're so right. I was a fool. But I've always been a bit of a coward . . .' he went on thoughtfully. 'Maybe because I wasn't tough enough.'

'You look it,' Simon said dryly.

Shawn laughed. 'I know. That's my defence. I look tougher than I am. At school I got really beaten up for I hated fighting. How about you, Simon?'

Simon hesitated. 'To be honest, Shawn, I was a coward too. Not exactly scared of being hurt but I hated violence. The sight of blood made me feel sick.' They all laughed. 'I know,' he said. 'Sounds crazy for a doctor. Maybe that's why I was one. To learn how to stop bleeding.'

'What made you be a doctor, Simon?' Cherry turned to him. 'I've always meant to

110

ask you.'

'Some other time, Cherry. We're there . . .' Simon said, drawing up outside the tall building.

'I'll walk in with you,' Shawn said. 'It's getting late.'

Cherry smiled up at him. 'Shawn, good luck . . .' she said earnestly. 'I'll keep my fingers crossed for you.'

They vanished into the house. Simon clenched his hands round the steering wheel. She hadn't even said goodnight to him! He meant nothing to her.

A wave of unusual anger swept through him. Anger with himself for his inadequacy, anger with Shawn for being everything he, Simon, would like to be.

Shawn could talk, laugh, make a girl feel relaxed and happy. Look how different Cherry had been that night? Never had she got so relaxed with him, Simon thought miserably. Shawn had that something a man needs, something lacking in himself, Simon realised.

Coming back to the car, Shawn slid in. 'Nice girl,' he said casually. 'Yours?'

Simon hesitated. He could lie and safeguard himself. Or . . .

'Not exactly,' he said honestly. 'Haven't known her long. She was walked out on just before they were to be married and she hates men.'

'I didn't get that impression.'

'She's getting over it,' Simon said quickly.

'So now what? First stop, police station?'

Simon hesitated. 'I'm afraid so. Like to stop for a drink first? A beer?'

'Sounds good to me but maybe we'd better not. Might influence them against me. Hell, Simon, I am sorry I got you involved,' Shawn said gravely.

'It's okay,' Simon told him. 'I know you didn't mean to and I think Cherry rather exaggerates.'

'She's always on the side of the one in trouble. Nice kid,' Shawn said. 'Like a cigarette? We were a bit squashed before.'

'Thanks. Shawn, I think . . .' He hesitated and took the cigarette, driving as slowly as he could along the front.

There was a round golden moon and all along the parade were dazzling coloured lights dangling from the lamp posts. 'Shawn,' he repeated, seeking for the right words. 'When you tell your story, I think you should mention your two bouts in hospital and the fact that you had concussion.'

'Isn't that being rather cowardly? Passing the buck? I mean I was in full possession of my senses.'

'But were you? Remember you said it was quite a party. Alcohol and concussion are not the best of friends.'

'But I'd drunk nothing the day I did it . . . No, that's a lie. I funked it so had two

112

brandies. Dad always said they soothed your nerves.'

'Why if you didn't want to, did you . . . well, do it?' Simon asked.

'Because I was a fool. Because I'm a show-off and I knew just what they'd say if I didn't. Laugh at me, Simon, as you like but I am a ridiculous sensitive creature and I hate being made to look . . . well, let's call it chicken.'

Simon drew up in the nearest parking place to the station. As they went into the building in the light, they stared at one another.

'Good luck,' Simon said.

'Thanks, mate,' Shawn's face was flushed. 'I'll need it.'

*   *   *

It was half an hour before Simon left the police station. Shawn was still being detained for questioning.

Simon had told Shawn how to find the house near Warrior Square.

'I've got to look in at the hospital first,' he said. 'But I expect I'll be home before you.'

'I'm sure you will,' the police sergeant had said dourly.

Simon went out to the car and started it. The police had been pleasant but rather unyielding. They thought it was a joke the two brothers had contrived and they didn't like jokes at their expense. They had pointed out the wasted time and tax-payers' money, that such similarity was unlikely to be natural: that they found it difficult to believe that the two brothers had never met since childhood till that evening.

Simon asked if Shawn would be detained.

'Not if you'll guarantee we can get in touch with him tomorrow,' the sergeant said. 'I'll expect he'll be wanted up there for further questioning.'

So Simon had got away and as he drove up London Road towards the hospital, he felt sorry for his brother. It was a damn stupid thing to have done, too childish for a man of thirty-three yet typical of so many groups of old school friends when they get together for a party. It wasn't a crime. Though it might have been serious. Driving into the hospital grounds, Simon wondered what the charge would have been had the teller been older and dropped dead. Manslaughter?

Mrs. Chester's eyes brightened as she saw him.

'I thought you'd forgotten me.'

He jerked forward a chair, turned it round and straddled it. 'My favourite patient?' he grinned. 'Not likely. How'd the journey go?'

'Fine. Just fine. The ambulance men were nice. Happen it's just women I don't get on with . . .' Mrs. Chester looked thoughtful. She leaned forward to hiss in Simon's ear. 'Don't you think the skirts are rather too short? Must

114

be distracting in the men's wards.' Then she giggled. 'Happen that's why they wear 'em short.'

Simon laughed with her. 'Happen it's a good idea.'

'You like them short? You got a girl?' Mrs. Chester asked. 'Whyn't you married, Doctor? A handsome young man like you? Got nervous feet? Ever been in love?'

'Often.' Simon relaxed. It was good to know there was no hurry and a short talk might help Mrs. Chester to go to sleep. Not a very pleasant time awaited her the next day, he knew. Tests could be boring as well as unpleasant. But she was tough so the odds were on her side. She stood far more chances of recovery than the average woman of her age.

'I'm sure you've often been in love, Mrs. Chester. There's a wild look in your eyes.'

She laughed happily. 'I was a proper little flirt. I was. Always did like men best. I've been married four times you know.' Her face clouded. 'Four times I've buried a husband. Happen I'm too old to have another go.'

Simon whistled softly. At that moment, the night nurse came round and told him it was time Mrs. Chester went to sleep.

'I'll try to look in tomorrow,' Simon said, 'but can't promise for I may be on call.'

'I understand,' Mrs. Chester looked at him anxiously. 'I am going to be all right, doctor?'

'It's up to you, Mrs. Chester, and knowing you, I'd back you every time,' he said.

Her face brightened. 'Thanks, Doctor, thanks a ton.'

He walked out of the hospital slowly. She really was amazing.

Shawn was not waiting when Simon got home. Not that Simon had really expected him to be. As he put the key in the flat front door, he heard the telephone bell shrilling. He ran to answer it, in case it was urgent.

It was Cherry.

'Oh Simon, I've been so worried. I kept phoning and . . .'

Worried about Shawn! Simon tried to keep his voice steady.

'I've only just got back. I left Shawn at the station.'

'Why did you leave him? I mean, how'll he find his way to you . . .' Cherry asked anxiously.

'Shawn is thirty-three, Cherry, and it is a straightforward walk,' Simon said stiffly. 'I told him how to get here. They didn't need me and I had to go and see Mrs. Chester.'

'Mrs. Chester? Is she ill?'

'No more ill than she always is but we're trying to correct the condition. She's in hospital and tomorrow they'll be . . . well, taking tests. I just went to chat her up a bit . . .'

'How sweet of you, Simon.'

'Well, you did point out to me how thoughtless and selfish I was,' Simon reminded her dryly, 'so I'm trying to reform.'

'Simon, I didn't really mean it . . . I was . . . well . . .'

'Emotionally disturbed?'

'That's right.'

He gave a little laugh. 'So you took it out on me.'

'Of course. We always have to have a whipping boy. Simon, what d'you think they'll do to Shawn?'

'I haven't a clue.' All Cherry thought of was Shawn, he told himself angrily. And she'd only known him a few hours! 'Anyhow he can come back here for the night and tomorrow has to go to town to answer more questions.'

'Did they make a big thing of it? I mean, is it a sort of crime?'

'Sort of . . . I suppose you could say. If the teller had died of shock, I suppose it could have been manslaughter.'

'Oh no. Poor Shawn.'

'What about the poor teller?'

'Of course, I mean the poor teller, too, but Shawn didn't mean to hurt anyone and . . .'

'It was lucky for him that he didn't.' Simon was getting more and more annoyed with her defence of Shawn. It could only mean . . . His mind shied away from the thought. Yet the fear remained.

'When will Shawn be back?' Cherry asked.

'I haven't a clue.'

'Well, I can't sleep until I know so would

you ask him to ring me, Simon?'

'Certainly,' he said. 'With the greatest pleasure I'll tell him,' he added sarcastically. 'He may be very late, of course, but I'll leave a note on the table.'

'You won't go to bed? He'll need someone to talk to . . .'

'He can talk to you. I'm tired and have a busy day tomorrow.' He put down the receiver carefully, afraid if he didn't, he might say something he would later regret.

Never before, not even when he thought he was in love with Alicia, had he felt this frightening flood of jealousy.

He went to the kitchen and made coffee. Then braced it with brandy. He found himself drumming his fingers on the table as he sat by the window, looking out at the moon-splashed sea. Despite what he had said to Cherry, Simon knew he could not go to bed until Shawn arrived.

At last he did. Stumbling up the stairs, knocking gently on the door. He looked pale and exhausted.

'Phew . . . your police can talk!' He sank into a chair and took a strong drink from Simon with gratitude. 'Sorry I've kept you up.'

'That's okay.' Simon straddled a chair and stared at him. 'How'd it go?'

'Not too bad. Pretty scathing, though. Said a party was no excuse for behaving like a moron. By the way what does that word mean?'

Simon grinned. 'An adult with a seven year old's mental development.'

Shawn laughed. 'They weren't far wrong. What fascinates them, though, is our likeness. Said we'd make a good couple for crime, standing in with our different alibis. Anyhow it wasn't as bad as I expected but I've got to go up tomorrow. They'll fetch me.'

'Hungry?'

'I'm starving.'

'Bread and cheese is all I've got.'

'Suit me fine . . . Can I help?'

Simon laughed. 'No. just relax. I've made some coffee. That reminds me. Cherry is anxious about you. She asked me to ask you to phone her as she can't go to sleep until she knows you're okay.'

Shawn looked surprised. 'Well now, I call that real nice of her. What's the number?'

Simon told him and then went out to the kitchen. Feeling ashamed of himself, he left the door open so that bits of what Shawn said drifted out as Simon cut hunks of bread and cheese and put them on plates.

'. . . not too bad. No, Cherry, I don't think so. Yes . . . tired but . . . Oh. Cherry, I'll be okay. Thanks all the same. Yes, Simon's here. Getting me something to eat. Answering questions makes me hungry. Thanks. Okay. Sure I will. 'Night . . .'

Shawn had just finished talking when Simon took in the tray of food, and cups of steaming coffee.

'Nice kid,' Shawn said. 'But don't girls flap. Anyone would think I was heading for the gallows.'

'She's got a vivid imagination.'

Shawn laughed. 'You're telling me. And a lot of other things. Ah well. We'll see what happens. Thanks for the grub, Simon. It looks swell.'

'I must say I'm hungry, too,' Simon said.

They ate in silence. When they had finished, Simon collected the china and carried it to the kitchen. He returned with sheets, pillows and blankets.

'Afraid I haven't a second bed. Can you manage on the couch?'

Shawn took the blankets. 'I can sleep on a floor. One thing I won't need rocking tonight.'

Simon looked at him sharply. 'You don't sleep well?'

'Not very. Takes ages for me to fall off to sleep and then I get nightmares.' Shawn bent over the couch, getting it ready then straightened and looked at Simon. 'You're right. I can see what you're thinking. Father.'

'But it wasn't your fault.'

Shawn straightened a blanket and looked Simon in the eyes. 'I know but what makes it worse is the fact I wanted him to die.'

'You . . . wanted . . . ?'

Shawn nodded. 'Not that he worried me so much for I was mostly away but I was so darn sorry for my step-mother and her kids. Not that I'd have killed him or anything but I remember thinking as I drove, how much simpler life would be for Maggie, that's my step-mother, if something happened to my father, And then . . . well, then it happened.'

He straightened. 'Simon, I'm always hearing talk about psychic things and extrasensory what-have-yous. Could my thought have caused the trailer to be let loose?'

'I'm sure it couldn't. You told me yourself the chain was rusted. Anyone could have been in the car behind the trailer and got killed. You've got what is generally called a guilt complex. Most people have one if someone near to them dies. Usually the guilt side of it is ludicrous. Yours is. If it gets no better, might be an idea to . . .'

'Go to a psychiatrist.'

'Yes. I mean if you're going to go on believing in your subconscious, if not your conscious, that your thought killed your . . . I mean *our* father, then you might as well go one step farther and start digging pins in small images of your enemies.'

'I guess you're right. Anyhow I doubt if I'll dream tonight. I'm really bushed.'

'So am I.' Simon laughed. 'By the way, if Mrs. Edwards—she's my housekeeper—lets out a yell when she sees you in the morning, don't worry. She's apt to be melodramatic at times and the sight of you on the couch may alarm her.'

'She doesn't know about me?'

'Of course not. I didn't—until a few hours ago. 'Night.'

Shawn yawned. ' 'Night . . .' he said and Simon went into his bedroom, closing the door.

He didn't go into bed at once. He stood by the window, staring blindly at the illuminated street. Had he missed his chance with Cherry by his own stupidity? Being *patient*? Shawn had got farther with Cherry in a few hours than Simon had in two months. What was it Shawn had that *he* lacked, Simon asked himself. Maybe if it had been Shawn in love with Alicia, she might not have walked out on him. But that was long gone past and, thanks be, it no longer hurt to remember Alicia.

But now, it was beginning to hurt when he remembered Cherry. Had Shawn already won? Was there still a chance?

Sighing, he got into bed, switching off the light. The phone extension by his bed rang shrilly. Silently cursing, Simon answered it. It was one of his patients asking him to come at once.

'I know you're not on call tonight, Doctor, but I'm feeling so terribly ill, I made them call you. The other doctor came earlier and gave me some pills but the pain is still there. I'm . . .' His voice rose.

'I'll be right over,' Simon promised, sliding

out of bed, hastily dressing.

Shawn looked up sleepily. 'A patient?' he said and yawned. 'Who'd be a doctor?' he asked and turned over.

Who, indeed, Simon thought as he hurried down the stairs. And then grinned at himself. It had been his own choice and though at times like these, when he could hardly keep awake, he mentally cursed himself for his foolishness, yet he knew that if he had to choose again, he'd make the same choice.

CHAPTER EIGHT

It was absurd. Childish, ridiculous! Something to be ashamed of, Simon told himself. But all the scolding, lecturing, hours of self-examination did not help. He became more and more conscious of the fact that he bitterly resented Shawn's powers of charm, that Shawn's entry into his life had caused him to feel jealous, envious and . . . Well, of course, it wasn't Shawn's fault. If anyone was at fault, Simon knew, it was himself. Somewhere or other along the way he had failed.

Shawn was rather sleepy that first day as they shared breakfast. But he was chuckling.

'Your Mrs. Edwards just stared at me as if I was something the cat found in the dustbin. 'But Doctor, what on earth are you . . .' she began and then you opened the door and stood there. You should have seen her face. It was as if she'd seen a ghost.'

'I'm not surprised,' Simon said, glancing at his watch, 'When did they say they'd come for you?'

The phone bell rang. Simon answered it. It was Cherry.

'Have they taken Shawn away yet?' she asked anxiously.

Simon had drawn a deep breath. 'Not yet. D'you want to talk to him?'

'If you don't mind Simon.'

'Of course not,' he said. But suppose he had told her that he did mind; that he minded very much indeed? He wondered what she would say, how she would react. Instead he called Shawn, who stumbled over half asleep, yawning.

'Hi, Cherry. What's wrong?' Shawn asked. Then laughed. 'Thanks. I may need it. Yes, of course I will. I'll phone Simon. What? Yes, I have got it. Okay, I'll phone you, too. What I'll do? If I'm let off, you mean? Well, I thought I'd go and stay a while in Brighton and get to know Aunt Flo. She seems a real peach . . . Yes, I do agree. Yes, it must be. That's the tragedy of growing old. They have too much time in which to do nothing and we have too little time in which to do everything . . .'

Simon had stood up, gulping down his coffee, so angry he could not have answered if spoken to. He was sure that Cherry was telling Shawn how terribly Simon had neglected poor Aunt Flo and how nice it would be for the old lady to have someone visit her.

Shawn hung up, finally, and turned. Simon looked at him coldly. 'I must be off. Hope things'll be all right. You'll keep in touch?'

'Sure.' Shawn looked a little puzzled. 'Something wrong?'

Simon managed a smile. He could hardly tell Shawn the truth!

'Just a bit tired. Bad night. However, good luck. Be seeing you.'

'And that's no lie,' Shawn grinned, holding out his hand. 'Now I've found myself a brother, I don't want to lose touch.'

So Simon had hurried down to the surgery and rung the bell for the first patient. Slowly the morning dragged by. He found himself wondering if the police had come and it was quite a shock when about quarter to twelve, the receptionist said there was a personal call for him, should she put it through.

Wondering if it could be Shawn so quickly, Simon said yes. In a moment he was speaking to Aunt Flo!

'Simon, dear boy. I'm worried about Shawn. Any news yet?' she asked.

It was the first time she had phoned Simon!

'No. Not really, Aunt Flo,' Simon kept his voice steady. 'He's had to go to London to answer questions but they seemed to be treating him well. Not that he's got much leg to stand on. It was the most idiotic . . .'

'I agree, dear boy, but we all do foolish things at times,' she said gently. 'He spent the night with you?'

'Yes. He's going to get in touch with you, Aunt Flo. Said he might come and stay in Brighton for a while.'

'Oh, that would be lovely. He is a darling, isn't he? So like you and yet so different, dear boy. You two got on well, didn't you?'

'Yes, fine. Cherry likes him, too,' Simon said.

'I'm sure she does. How could anyone dislike him.' Aunt Flo said. 'Well, dear boy, I know you're busy so I'll hang up but if you hear anything about Shawn, you will let me know?'

'Of course, Aunt Flo, of course.' Simon put down the receiver very gently, afraid that the sudden spurt of anger in him might make him slam it down and break it. This new anger of his!

His lunch hour was disturbed by another phone call. Cherry this time.

'No, I haven't heard from him,' Simon said slowly. trying to hide his irritation. 'He'll let us know as soon as there is anything to know.'

'They won't keep him?'

'How do I know, Cherry? They may retain him or let him out on bail. It all depends. I don't know what the procedure is in a case like

126

this. No, I shouldn't think they'd be very harsh. I mean, it is a first offence and though very childish, he . . .'

'He didn't mean to hurt anyone.'

'No one does yet it's easy to if you don't think . . .' Simon said, his irritability beginning to show. The way to win a girl's love and an old lady's admiration seemed to be to do something as stupid as Shawn had done. You could lead a normal, almost perfect life and no one even *saw* you, let alone fell in love with you. The whole thing was crazy.

'Well . . .' Cherry hesitated as if she'd got the message and knew Simon was fed-up. 'I expect he'll let us know.'

'I expect so,' Simon said dully and hung up.

On his round, he was asked again and again about his twin brother. There had been a brief paragraph in the morning paper, saying that Dr. Britten had been questioned by mistake and that the real S. Britten had gone to the police voluntarily to assist them.

'And you didn't know you had a twin brother?'

'Are you so alike?'

'It must be exciting to find you've got a brother.'

'Is he a doctor, too?'

Questions and comments all the time. And always, Simon thought bitterly, about his wonderful brother, Shawn! No one asked about Simon, or how he had liked being questioned by the police because of something his brother had done. No one was interested in dull Simon . . .

That evening he dined with the Donwards. Cherry was there. Betsy wanted to know all about it.

'And what's happening to him?' she asked Simon.

'I haven't heard.'

Cherry leaned forward. 'He tried to get you but you were out so he phoned me. He's got to appear before the magistrate or something in two weeks. Meanwhile he's out on bail, I think, and has gone down to see your Aunt Flo, Simon.'

'I see.' Simon's face felt stiff, his mouth dry. 'Did they give him any idea what will happen?'

'Not exactly but they hinted it would probably be a fine and an admonishment. What a word . . .' Cherry said and they all laughed.

Simon never knew how he endured that evening. All the time it was Shawn, Shawn, Shawn. Cherry did most of the talking for Simon had unconsciously withdrawn into a shell and just nodded if they asked him if he agreed. Cherry told them Shawn's life history, his nightmares because of his father's death and his feeling of guilt, and why he had done such a stupid thing.

'I think the nicest thing about Shawn is his absolute honesty,' Cherry said, her cheeks flushed, her eyes shining. She was looking particularly attractive in a salmon-pink cat-suit, her hair brushed back from her forehead for once, the curls tied up like a pony tail. Simon had never heard her speak so happily.

'Shawn admits he is chicken when the boys start bullying. I think that takes courage. To admit it, I mean. He's so completely without inhibitions. I wonder if all Australians are like that.'

Simon found his voice. 'I thought Shawn said he was very English.'

Cherry turned to him eagerly. 'He would be—in Australia—but he isn't very English here, is he?'

'Isn't he?' Simon stared at her coldly. 'What would you call very English here?'

There was surprise in Cherry's eyes. 'You must know, Simon, for you're very English. The men are much quieter, they don't boast or show-off, and they're very reserved and even sometimes scared.'

Paul shouted with laughter. 'That's not a bad description of you, Simon, old chap.'

Simon found it hard to sit still and join in the laughter. Never, but never in his whole life, had he hated anyone as much as he hated Shawn at that moment.

He thought, at times, the evening would never end. He drove Cherry home silently. When he walked into the building with her to say goodbye, she looked up at him worriedly.

'Are you all right, Simon?'

'Of course I'm all right,' he said irritably. 'Why shouldn't I be?'

'I don't know. Just that you . . . well, you're not like you, tonight.'

'Aren't I? Maybe because I'm dead tired. I had a late night last night for I was called out . . .'

'But you weren't on call, Simon.'

'I know but this particular man . . . well, he needs reassurance or he'll just let go. I often have to slip round to see him and then the pain goes. Purely . . .'

'Fear?'

He frowned. 'Not fear but uncertainty, lack of security. Some illnesses give you that.'

'Not only illness,' Cherry said.

Simon hesitated. 'You mean . . . unhappy love affairs? Yes, they do damage the ego, don't they.'

'And how,' Cherry said, her voice thick. ' 'Night, Simon,' she added, and slipped away.

He watched her go up the first flight and then he turned, walking back to the car. Oddly enough his ego had been more damaged by his twin brother, Shawn than the heartbreak caused by Alicia. What was it Shawn had that he lacked? Simon asked himself again and again.

The next lunch hour, Betsy Donward phoned him.

'What was wrong with you last night,

Simon?'

'Wrong with me? Nothing.' Instinctively he had stiffened warily. 'What could be wrong?'

'The way you behaved. Almost as if you dislike poor Cherry. I could see how upset she was.'

'Cherry? Why, I thought I'd never seen her look so happy.'

'You must need your eyes testing, Simon,' Betsy teased. 'All the same, you weren't yourself. Even Paul, our dear Paul . . .' she chuckled, 'who is as blind as a bat as regards temperaments and moods said there was something wrong with you. You didn't let that stupid mistake get you down, did you?'

'Stupid mistake?'

'Yes, when you were mistaken for your brother and had the photo in the paper.'

'No. That didn't worry me at all.'

'Then, Simon, what is it? The way you said *that* betrayed you.' She laughed. 'Come clean, Simon. What's biting you?'

He hesitated. 'If I tell you, swear you won't tell Paul? He'd never stop teasing me.'

'I swear . . .' Betsy said dramatically.

Simon found himself able to laugh. 'Well, it's so childish that I'm almost ashamed to tell you.'

'The nicest people are children at heart, Simon.'

He felt himself relaxing still more. 'Well, you're going to laugh like mad but I . . . I was

131

just plain jealous.'

Betsy didn't laugh. 'That's not like you, Simon,' she said gravely.

'I know. The first time I can remember feeling like this.'

'Jealous of whom? Shawn?'

'Exactly. My own brother.'

'Well, Simon, you can hardly expect to feel brotherly love for him overnight. But why you should be jealous . . .'

'Look . . . well . . . in a way . . .' Simon stumbled among the words. 'I know it's absurd, Betsy, but in a few hours, he got further with Cherry than I have in weeks. He's got a charm with him . . .'

'Only because he doesn't love her,' Betsy said quietly.

Simon caught his breath. 'I don't understand.'

'The point is, you do, don't you, Simon? That was obvious from the word go. The love you feel for Cherry means you have walked carefully, knowing she was recovering from a broken heart but, Simon, there are times when slow walking can be carried too far.'

'I've wondered that sometimes,' he admitted. 'But I'd hate to catch her on the rebound. That never works.'

'No, but you can still build up a foundation friendship.'

'I've tried, Betsy. That's why I asked you to ask us to dinner but now she never stops talking about Shawn.'

'She had to talk about something, poor girl. You sat there, looking like Lot's wife after she had turned to stone.'

'I did?' Simon was startled. 'Well, I'm sorry about that. What can I do?'

'Send her a bunch of flowers. It's her birthday on Saturday. You might get her a small bottle of expensive scent. Every girl likes that. But make it small otherwise she'll be embarrassed. And a birthday card. Then I'll ask you both to dinner again but with a young couple to keep the conversation flowing. Where is this brother of yours now?'

'I think he's going to stay in Brighton to see Aunt Flo.'

'I suppose you're jealous of that.'

Simon laughed. 'I'll confess. I am.'

'You men!' Betsy sighed. 'I can't understand you. Why won't you see that a woman can love in many different ways. The love Aunt Flo has for you could never be equalled by the love she has for Shawn. She's sorry for his long years of not being loved, years in which *you* have been loved. The trouble is, Simon, you've been shockingly spoiled.'

'That's what Cherry said,' Simon admitted meekly.

Betsy laughed. 'Well, you're still very nice but the trouble is that you're scared of losing what in the past you've taken for granted. The point to remember, Simon, is that love never dies. Unless you do something really terrible to kill it. You couldn't. So let poor Shawn have a bit of the love he needs and try to like him.'

'Actually I do. It was just this . . .'

'Well, it might be an idea to let Cherry see you're jealous. Girls thrive on that so long as you don't carry it to extremes. I mean, don't get possessive and suspect her every time she smiles at Shawn but let her see you like to have her alone and without Shawn hanging around. Look, Simon, didn't you tell me your Aunt Flo has a pretty girl looking after her? Yes? I thought so. Well, what're you worrying about? Shawn will probably fall for her if he's the sort of Don Juan Cherry called him.'

Simon smiled. 'Thanks a lot, Betsy. I feel better for having wept on your shoulder. Sorry, if I bored you.'

'On the contrary. When you reach my advanced age . . .' She chuckled, knowing that to Simon at thirty-three, her forty-eight years made her an 'oldie', 'it is flattering to have a handsome young man confide in you. Now don't forget. Saturday is Cherry's birthday.'

'No. I won't. Thanks.' Simon put down the receiver gently. He stretched his arms, yawning. He felt much better. Now he saw his stupid jealousy in the right perspective. He felt excited. Betsy wouldn't be encouraging him like this if she hadn't an idea . . . He wondered if perhaps Cherry confided in her.

He whistled as he ran down the stairs,

glancing at his watch. He had time to stop in town to order some flowers. He wondered what kind. Red roses, he thought. Aunt Flo had told him once that red roses had always won a way to her heart.

Maybe, he told himself, as he slid behind the steering wheel, maybe he'd been making a mountain out of a molehill and perhaps he had a chance, after all.

CHAPTER NINE

Simon stopped outside the florist shop, parking his car, going in to look at all the flowers. Red roses was still his choice.

'You'd like to write a little note?' the girl in a green overall asked with a smile.

She gave him a card to be put in an envelope. Balancing it on his hand rather precariously, he wrote:

'Sorry about last night. Betsy says I was moody. Simon.'

He pushed it in the envelope, sealed it and wrote Cherry's name and address on it. The assistant told him how much it would cost and as he took the money from his pocket, Simon remembered something Betsy had once said about flowers:

That it was every woman's dream that she'd be sent flowers.

His mouth curled with amusement. Well, why not? As he was there!

He ordered sweet peas for Aunt Flo and scribbled a note. And then thought again. He wasn't sure if he'd be able to get to the hospital that day, so . . .

He ordered bright red gladioli for Mrs. Chester.

'Sorry I can't get to see you. Chin up,' he scribbled and wondered what the quiet, rather serious girl serving him would say if she could read what he had written. It wasn't every patient he could or would send flowers and write notes to, but Mrs. Chester was different. He admired her for her courage and constant cheerfulness.

Glancing at his watch, he paid the bill and hurried to his car, before starting on his afternoon round of visits. He whistled as he drove. Maybe Betsy was right and it *was* time to start wooing Cherry. He had no doubts as far as *he* was concerned. He'd loved her from the word go. Ever since that day when she had been so unfriendly and had called him selfish, and goodness knows what else! His only anxiety was about the man she had loved. Had she forgotten him? Yet?

The next morning, he had a phone call from Aunt Flo.

'Dear boy, how nice of you to send me flowers. You remembered I always loved sweet peas. It's so unlike you, though, Simon. I mean, sending me flowers. I can't ever remember you doing it before. What made you, dear boy?'

'Well . . .' Simon hesitated. 'I was there in the flower shop and I remembered something Betsy Donward had said about every woman longing to be sent flowers. So . . . so I sent you some.'

'She is right, dear boy. It was a delightful surprise. What were you doing in a flower shop?'

Again he hesitated. 'Well, honestly, Aunt Flo, it seems that the other night at the Donwards' house, I behaved badly.'

'You did?' She sounded shocked. 'I find that hard to believe. Your manners are impeccable, dear boy.'

'According to Betsy, they weren't. I wasn't aware of it myself but Betsy said I was moody.' He chuckled. 'She even said I acted like Lot's wife.'

'Lot's wife? Oh! The woman who looked back when she was told not to and was turned to stone? I'm afraid I would have done the same. I can't bear to be told not to do a thing. So . . .?'

'Well,' Simon wondered if he was saying too much but now he'd got so far . . . 'Betsy said I was rude to Cherry . . .'

'To Cherry? Oh, no! How could you be rude to Cherry?' Aunt Flo asked.

'I didn't know it and I certainly didn't mean

137

to be rude to her but Betsy said I was and . . . well, she suggested flowers so I sent them. I'm also getting her a small present for her birthday. Cherry's, I mean.'

'Is her birthday soon?'

'Saturday, She's thirty. Betsy told me once that this is the most frightening age for any woman. Would you agree?'

There was silence. Obviously Aunt Flo had to think.

'Could be she's right, Simon. Especially when you're not married. It is alarming, gives you a feeling you're going to be left on the shelf. Forty isn't very nice, either. Fifty . . . well, that's not easy. Sixty didn't worry me at all. I knew I was still young as compared to eighties and nineties. I find the older I grow the less age worries me. After all, it's how you feel not how many years you've lived that counts. I wouldn't have thought Cherry was that old, Simon. She looks about twenty, if that.'

'All the girls do today, Aunt Flo. Including the old girls.' He laughed. 'You certainly don't look your age.'

'Thank you, dear boy. How very comforting to be told that. So Cherry's birthday is on Saturday. Are you taking her out to dinner?'

'I hadn't thought of that. When I asked her before, she kept digging up lame excuses.'

'But you do know her better now, don't you?'

Simon smiled. 'You're so right, Aunt Flo. I do and I will.'

'Dear lad. She's a sweet girl. By the way, Simon, Shawn asked me to . . . well, give you his love.'

Simon stiffened, quite unaware that his tone became different, cold and wary. 'He's with you?'

'Well, not exactly. He's staying at a hotel but spends most of the day with us.'

'That must be nice,' Simon said.

'It is dear boy, very nice. Not often I have two young people with me.'

'Two?'

'Of course. You've forgotten Teresa. She's given up her work and is looking after me all the time, now. It is such a comfort having a young person around and she is so good.'

'I'm glad, Aunt Flo.'

'Dear boy, I want to thank you for her.'

'Please Aunt Flo, you know how it embarrasses me and . . .'

'Yes Simon dear. I do know. All the same, thank you. Teresa is making a great difference to my life. Now I really must go. 'Bye dear boy.'

He put down the receiver slowly and looked up as Anne Wallace, the receptionist who still irritated him, came into the room.

'While you were on the phone, a call came through the other line from the hospital. Mrs. Chester, apparently is worse and Dr. Donward thought you could help.'

Simon stood up quickly. 'Of course. How many in the waiting room?'

'Two for you but I could pass them on to Dr. Daniels.'

'Yes, please do . . .' he said curtly.

He drove as fast as he could despite the growing summer traffic to the hospital. Paul came to meet him.

They talked briefly and then Paul left him. Simon stood by the side of Mrs. Chester's bed. Curtains had been drawn round it. Her face was pale and drawn, the skin stretched tautly over the cheekbones. He sat down by her side. She looked asleep, lying very still, eyes closed. On the locker by her side were the red gladioli glorious in their colour.

Simon took the old lady's hand in his. It was limp, the fingers flopping. But she opened her eyes and moved her mouth.

He bent down to hear what she said:

'I am so happy, Doctor.' She gave a faint smile. 'All my life I dreamt—happen one day I'd be sent some flowers. Happen someone will like me enough . . .'

Her eyes filled with tears. Slowly they trickled down her pale cheeks. Then she smiled:

'Thank you young man. Thank you . . .' she whispered and then turned her head away, closing her eyes.

He sat by her side, holding her hand. Ten

minutes later, he stood up, bent over her, looking at her eyes, feeling her wrist. Then he went outside to the Ward Sister.

She was young with fair hair escaping under the starched cap. There was a question in her eyes and she saw the answer in his.

'At least she died happy . . .' the Sister said. 'Those flowers you sent her, Doctor. She cried and when I went to see what was wrong, she told me that . . .'

Simon's face burned. 'I know. She told me. Look . . .'

'It was . . . what we thought it was?' the Sister asked.

'Yes. The tests, I gather, showed that.'

'She must have suffered a lot of pain.'

'She was a brave old girl.'

'And a real tartar,' the Sister said with a faint smile. 'Still, I was lucky this time. She didn't throw soup over me.'

Simon walked down the many steps slowly. He shook his head as if he was—as he was—puzzled. Who'd ever thought a bunch of flowers would mean so much to an old woman of seventy-nine?

Saturday was a sunny day and Simon, being off duty for the weekend, went into town to buy a *small* bottle of scent. It was a difficult choice to make. The girl behind the counter, dark hair piled high, a bright smile pinned patiently to her face, advised and advised him, giving him samples to smell but each time he shook his head.

'That isn't her.'

'Well, what is she like?' the exasperated girl asked finally.

Simon half shut his eyes. 'Well, she's got red hair and green eyes and four freckles on her nose and . . . and . . .'

'We have one you might like. It's called *L'Aimant* . . .' the assistant said with a suppressed smile, as she offered a small bottle.

He smelt it and nodded at once. 'That's it. It is fresh yet . . . yet exciting, if you know what I mean.'

The girl smiled. 'Yes, I do.'

Lucky girl whoever the red-head was, she thought, as she did up the small bottle. He certainly was crazy over her.

Simon went into another shop and carefully chose a birthday card. He felt a little embarrassed though why he should, he had no idea. For all those smiling assistants knew, he might have been choosing a birthday card for Aunt Flo. At least he found the one he wanted. It looked right somehow.

Next he drove to the block of flats by the Green. Feeling absurdly nervous, for perhaps their whole future depended on his reception, he rang the bell.

Cherry answered it. She was wearing a pale green towelling coat, had bare feet, and half her hair was in rollers.

'I've just washed my hair . . .'

'I'm sorry if . . .'

She opened the door wide. 'Of course not. Come in. Heather is out at the moment, shopping for us. You don't mind if I finish my hair?'

'Of course not.' He followed her into the room and looked round curiously. It was a pleasant room, showing the inhabitants were two girls inclined to be untidy, for a sewing machine was on a table, some material spread out over the floor with a paper pattern strewn over it, a folding mirror on the sideboard, and comb and rollers beside it. Yellow curtains and a rather faded brown carpet, with several aged-looking armchairs. Into one of which, he sank. Of course Cherry and her friend were renting the flat furnished, he reminded himself.

He waited while she hastily finished her hair, combing it and putting the rollers on. She turned and gave him a rueful smile.

'Sorry I look such a fright.'

'I'm sorry I came so early only I wanted to . . .'

She came to sit on the edge of a chair opposite him.

'Wanted to . . .?'

He held out the small parcel and envelope. 'Happy birthday, Cherry.'

'Oh, Simon . . .' a pretty flush filled her cheeks. 'How very sweet of you.'

He looked round as she clumsily opened the parcel. Ah, his red roses were there. Standing

143

by the window, looking fresh and beautiful. He frowned as he noticed some yellow roses the other side of the room. They looked sad, wilting.

'Simon, *L'Aimant*, how lovely . . .' Cherry was undoing the bottle sniffing the perfume. 'It's perfect.' She looked up at him, her eyes bright. 'How did you know it was my birthday?' She smiled. 'Actually I was going to forget it. I'm thirty, you know.'

He laughed. 'I know but you don't look it. Aunt Flo said the same.'

'Did she? I wonder if that explains a mystery, Simon.' Cherry jumped up, went to the sideboard and opened a drawer.

She came back with a small, very pretty silver-trimmed evening bag. 'Shawn sent me that. I wondered how he knew it was my birthday. If I'd known you knew, I'd have thought it telepathy, unconscious, perhaps, but . . .'

'He must have got it from Aunt Flo,' Simon said, his voice dull. 'I told her yesterday.'

'Oh that explains it . . .' Cherry smiled. 'That reminds me, Simon. Thanks for those lovely golden roses.'

'Golden . . .?' Simon sat up quickly, frowning. 'But I ordered red roses. I thought those . . .' He looked at the beautiful ones by the window.

'Those came from Shawn,' Cherry said.

Simon bit his lip as he tried to control his

144

anger. 'I particularly said I wanted red roses . . .'

'They came from the same shop, Simon. Shawn's came early, sometime in the morning. Interflora . . . you know what I mean, ordered from another town. Maybe the assistant decided that as I'd already had red flowers, yellow roses would make a change. I love them.'

'I'm glad,' Simon sat back, he felt limp and discouraged. Shawn seemed to be a jump ahead of him all the time. Betsy had said a small present but that evening bag Cherry obviously liked so much must have cost five times what the perfume had.

Cherry was stroking the handbag gently. She looked up. 'Shawn is a scream. Know what he wrote with the bag? He said he hoped one day I'd use it when I went out dancing with him. He's got a nerve.' She laughed. 'He seems to think that every girl falls for him. A fast worker.'

Simon took a deep breath. 'Is that so bad?' he asked stiffly. 'Moving so fast, I mean.' He looked at his hands, clasped before him as he leaned forward, legs apart.

So he didn't see the strange look Cherry gave him. 'Sometimes it's better than moving too slowly . . .' Cherry said, her voice sharp. 'At least, moving fast gets you somewhere . . .'

Startled, Simon looked up. They stared at one another for a moment. Simon thought fast. What did she mean by that? Was it a hint?

A subtle reproof? Was he being too cautious?

He opened his mouth to speak and closed it again for the door opened, and a tall thin girl in tight black trews and a white shirt, her fair hair tied back with a white ribbon, came into the room and put a full basket on the table.

'There. Now we shouldn't starve,' she said.

Cherry jumped up. 'Heather, I want you to meet Simon, Dr. Britten.'

The girl's face changed, became interested instead of fed-up.

'Dr. Britten?' She held out her hand. 'Hi. I've heard a lot about you.'

'Have you? Complimentary things, I trust?' he said and thought how pompous it sounded.

She grinned. 'Wouldn't you like to know,' she teased. She picked up the basket. 'I'll put the stuff away. How's the hair going Cherry? Only I'll want the dryer soon . . .'

'I shan't be long. In a moment . . .' Cherry began.

Simon stood up. He could take a hint as well as anyone! As they walked to the door, he remembered something he had nearly forgotten. He stopped so suddenly that Cherry, following close behind, bumped into him and, for a moment he caught hold of her as he steadied her.

'Sorry but I nearly forgot. Would you have dinner with me tonight?' he asked, his voice almost lifeless for he had no hope she would accept.

Instead she startled him. Her face lit up, her eyes shone.

'Why thanks Simon. I'd love to. Will you pick me up or shall I meet you in town?'

He was so taken aback that it took him a few seconds to grasp it. She said Yes! Yes! Yes!

'I'll fetch you. I thought we might go out in the country somewhere. Such nice days—light so late . . . I mean, some of those country hotels are very good.'

A little smile played round her mouth. 'Sounds super. What time?'

'About . . . about six?'

'Fine. See you then . . .' Cherry said and closed the door.

Simon ran down the stairs quickly. He couldn't believe it. She had accepted it without any hesitation. Did that mean anything?

CHAPTER TEN

It was a pleasant country hotel. They had driven out past Battle and come across it by chance. A huge horseshoe was the front doorway. Inside the restaurant was one glass wall showing a delightful garden of grass, flowering pink and white shrubs and several fountains on a central pool, where yellow lilies floated.

As they sat in the garden with their drinks

before they ate, Cherry, wearing a green dress with a darker green velvet belt, matched by the ribbons in her hair, smiled at Simon.

'What made Betsy think you were rude the other night?'

He twisted in his chair to look at her. 'I didn't mean to be if *you* thought I was, Cherry.'

'I didn't think you were *rude* but rather upset. I couldn't understand why.'

He shrugged, gesturing with his hands. 'I don't know why. I wasn't even aware that I was being difficult. Maybe it was because of Shawn . . .'

Cherry frowned. 'Shawn? What's he got to do with it?'

Simon leaned forward. 'Because I'm . . .' he began and the waiter came with two enormous menus.

'Would you care to order, sir?'

Frowning Simon agreed. Inside him, he cursed. He had just been going to tell the truth. That he was insanely jealous of his twin brother! And the . . . waiter!

'What would you like, Cherry?'

They settled in the end for prawn cocktails, then grilled sole, and finally strawberries and cream.

'But we're in no hurry,' Simon said, rather irritably.

'Of course not, sir, nor is there any need to hurry,' the waiter, tall, greying, and with a strange smile, said politely.

At last they were alone. At least, not really alone for there were groups of people sitting outside in the sunshine but Simon and Cherry were in a small alcove, surrounded and cut off from the others by beautifully trimmed cypress trees.

'You were saying *why* you were upset. Something to do with Shawn?' Cherry asked.

Simon sighed. The moment for truth had somehow gone.

'Well, let's face it, Cherry. It is rather a shock to know you have a twin brother for the first time.'

'I'd have thought it was groovy news. I wish I had a twin sister.'

'I think . . .' Simon said slowly. 'it was partly the shock about my father. You see Aunt Flo rarely talked about him. But when she did, she gave me the impression that my father was a wonderful man. I knew he had gone to Australia. I didn't know he saw me as the runt of the litter . . .' he added bitterly. 'Aunt Flo only told me when we went to Amsterdam.'

Cherry nodded. 'Go on,' she said gently.

'I was shocked to learn that my father never answered Aunt Flo's letters . . .'

'But he kept them,' Cherry pointed out. 'And they were opened. I'm sure that meant he read them. Perhaps he had a guilt complex about you?'

'Judging from what Shawn said, I shouldn't

149

think he remembered I had existed.'

Cherry looked at her hands. 'I think he should have remembered you in his Will.'

'If he read the letters he must have known I was a doctor so perhaps he thought I didn't need money.' It was inconsistent of him, Simon knew, yet he suggested this for somehow it was a comforting thought.

Cherry looked puzzled. 'And you think he thought Shawn *would* need it? Yet what about his wife and children?'

'I suppose he knew Shawn,' Simon said wearily. He was getting fed-up with his brother's name which constantly entered into the conversation, 'and so was sure that Shawn would look after them.'

'And you.'

Simon shook his head. 'I'm not taking money from Shawn. If my father didn't love me enough . . .'

'You'll upset Shawn if you refuse.'

'It'll upset me if I accept,' Simon said angrily and then he had to laugh. 'Look . . .' he said. 'Maybe we should go in now and eat.'

Cherry laughed, too, and stood up quickly as if relieved that the conversation was over.

Much later after eating a delectable meal as Simon called it, to be scolded laughingly by Cherry for talking so pedantically, they sat in a deep couch in the lounge, drinking coffee and liqueurs. Maybe the meal and the champagne Simon insisted on buying to celebrate Cherry's birthday, plus the hot sweet coffee and the rich liqueurs had erased his inhibitions for suddenly he found himself telling Cherry about Alicia.

'It took me five years to get over her,' he said wonderingly.

'She hurt you very much?' Cherry asked gently.

He nodded. 'I suppose I was a fool. But I always have taken what people say to be the truth. I thought she was the most beautiful, witty, intelligent and exciting girl in the world.' He gave a funny little laugh. 'I must have been crazy.'

'She wasn't?'

'No, she was the most one-minded, selfish, arrogant, impossible creature imaginable.'

Cherry laughed. 'You certainly seem to be cured.'

'Yes, I am. Ever since I . . .' Simon began and halted abruptly. This was surely not the right moment to tell Cherry he loved her? Not after just showing how he had completely learned to unlove Alicia.

'What happened?'

'Well, her parents liked me. Aunt Flo didn't like her but she never said so until long afterwards. Alicia liked the best of everything and I wanted to give her that. We were officially engaged, bought the ring, even chose the house we were going to live in. I'd been offered a good job at Oxford, research work which fascinated me. Salary good. I had friends there. Then . . . then . . .' He paused as a noisy group of people stood in the doorway looking into the almost empty lounge and then, joking and laughing, walked on to the full bar.

'Then?'

'I got a *dear John* letter, as they used to call them in the war, Aunt Flo says. In other words, Alicia wrote and told me she'd changed her mind. She had thought a lot and decided the life of a doctor's wife was not for her. She wanted to be first love in a man's life . . .'

'Wouldn't she have been?'

Simon looked at her. 'Of course not. A doctor's work always comes first. I suppose it's so in many cases. A policeman, for instance. But I'm always sorry for doctors' wives for they must find it so lonely, sitting at home, waiting . . .'

'If they've any sense,' Cherry said, 'they'd have some engrossing work, hobby or something. Like painting or music.'

'Wouldn't you hate it if you were giving a dinner party and at the last moment, your husband was called out?'

Cherry looked puzzled. 'Not particularly. It doesn't seem to worry Betsy.'

Simon drew a deep breath. One obstacle overcome. Cherry had said quite plainly that she would have no objection to marrying a doctor! One step forward.

152

'You were lucky, Simon,' Cherry said unexpectedly. 'At least you got a letter.'

'You didn't?'

'No the wedding was due in a week. I'm an orphan but lived with an aunt. She died soon after . . . after he went. I had no idea he was—well, going. He was his usual self the last time we went dancing together and then he vanished. I rang his firm and they said he'd handed in his resignation and walked out. No, they didn't know where he was . . . This went on and then one day I got a letter. Just an envelope addressed to me in his handwriting.' Her voice was unsteady as she went on.

'As I opened it, I didn't know how to feel. Was this an explanation, was he going to say he was sorry . . . or was it . . . honestly, Simon. I didn't know what to think. I could only hope.'

'You still loved him?'

'Of course. You did, too, didn't you? You can't switch off love just like that.'

'What was in the envelope?'

'A small newspaper cutting. It was the brief account of his wedding to a girl in a small town in Scotland. I didn't even know he knew any one up there. I had no idea . . .' she said, her voice quivering.

Simon put his hand over hers. 'The . . . sadist. He must have been unbalanced. That was a terrible thing to do.'

'He was always lazy about writing letters. I suppose he saw it as the simplest.' She didn't remove her hand from his. 'Seems like we're two of a kind, Simon. Both with broken hearts.'

'Oh, mine's cured. Completely,' Simon said quickly. 'Yours will be one day.'

'I suppose so. It might take an awful long time. You said it was five years ago and you're only just over it?'

'Yes but . . . but well, I hadn't met anyone I liked during all that time. It might have been different if I had. The trouble is, Cherry, that you have to watch out you're not caught on the rebound.'

'Rebound?'

'Yes, well, I mean . . . when you're hurt and . . . and all that and terribly lonely, it would be awfully easy to imagine you could marry someone kind, someone who . . . well, who was nice.'

'You mean, it would be easy to think you'd fallen in love?' Cherry said thoughtfully.

Simon nodded. 'Exactly. You see,' he turned sideways to look at her. She had tossed off her shoes, tucked her legs under her skirt. She looked grave.

'I don't know, Simon. Maybe men are different from girls. When you've loved someone so much, you can't just turn to the next one who happens to be nice and kind. You want more than that to fall in love . . .'

'I agree completely but you might *imagine* it was love,' Simon said quickly.

154

She looked at him and shook her head. 'When it's real love, you *know*.'

'Yes, yes, when it's real love but . . .'

'I should think five years is long enough . . .'

'I wasn't thinking of . . .' Simon began.

The waiter was there, collecting the empty cups and glasses. 'Anything else, sir?' he asked politely.

Simon sighed, looking at his watch. 'No, thanks. Good grief, Cherry, I had no idea it was so late. We'd better go . . .'

They walked out into the warm night. When they were nearly back in St. Leonards, Simon took a long deep breath. Ever since they left the hotel, Cherry had talked of Shawn. 'Shawn said this . . .' 'Shawn did that . . .' 'Shawn says . . .' she had chattered on and on, always about Shawn.

He'd had enough, Simon decided. Shawn was always there to come intruding on them. If only Cherry could forget Shawn. Was Betsy completely wrong in what she had said? He thought so. Surely no girl could talk so much of a man unless she liked him? Or perhaps even more than liked him?

He listened silently, finding it hard not to shout at her to stop talking about his brother.

And then suddenly, he realised something. He was giving up without a fight, or even an attempt at a fight. Was he going to sit back quietly and let Shawn win her, only, perhaps, to break her heart for it was obvious that

Shawn fell in and out of love. No, Simon decided. This he could not allow. He loved Cherry too much . . . He'd fight for her.

'Cherry, I'm off duty and the weather seems good so I wondered if you'd like us to go for a drive tomorrow. Take a picnic lunch?'

Cherry turned eagerly. 'That would be lovely, Simon. It seems a shame to waste this gorgeous sunshine.'

'Good. D'you like to sleep late on Sundays? What time shall I pick you up? About ten . . . eleven?'

She laughed. 'Make it twelve. I love to read the newspapers in bed on Sunday. My treat of the week. I was wondering . . .' She hesitated, watching him carefully. 'I was wondering if we could visit Aunt Flo. She does so enjoy seeing you . . .'

Simon, whose blood had began to race happily at her immediate acceptance of his invitation, felt himself turning cold. So it was Shawn. That could be the only reason she wanted to go to Brighton. Why, she hardly knew Aunt Flo! It was always Shawn, Shawn, Shawn . . . !

And then he remembered something else. Teresa.

Now Teresa was no ordinary girl. Not only was she rather a dish, as Paul would call her, but intelligent, friendly and vulnerable. Judging from what Betsy had said, men like Shawn couldn't help chatting up every pretty girl they saw. Suppose if they went to Brighton and Cherry saw Shawn making a pass at Teresa, it would make her realise the kind of man he was and help her realise that with Shawn, there could only be heartbreak.

'Of course,' Simon, said cheerfully. 'A good idea. I suggest we have a picnic lunch on the way so that Aunt Flo won't be flapping about her guests. She does flap, you know, though of course now she has Teresa with her . . .'

'Teresa seems a nice girl?' Cherry asked rather than said.

'Very nice indeed. I'm sorry for her. Just lost her mother, you know.'

'Very tough.' Cherry said and closed her eyes. She had loved her aunt, too, even though most of her youth she had been passed from one relative to the next, Aunt Gay had been the chief woman in her life.

'I wonder if Shawn will be there,' Simon said as casually as he could.

'Why don't you like him, Simon?'

The unexpected question from Cherry startled him.

'Like . . .? Yes, of course I like him. The little I've seen of him . . . well . . .'

'The plain truth is, you're jealous. Aren't you, Simon?'

They had reached the Green and he parked outside her block of flats. Now he turned to her, taken aback by the truthful words. Was it so obvious?

Hadn't Betsy told him to let Cherry know he was jealous? And that every girl liked that sort of jealousy provided it didn't go to extremes?

'Yes. I am jealous . . .' he said suddenly.

Cherry opened the car door. 'How can you be so mean, Simon Britten,' she said angrily. 'I can't understand your make-up. You're just plain selfish. Begrudging poor Shawn the little love Aunt Flo can give him now when you've had so much all your life. Have you any idea what it's like to grow up, knowing that no one really loves you? I do. My relations were kind but no one really cared. Not even my aunt. Not really. Not love as Aunt Flo gave you.'

She paused for breath but rushed on without giving him a chance to speak.

'Can't you see or won't you see, what's wrong with Shawn? He needs love . . .'

'Don't we all?' Simon said bitterly. What was the good of trying? Shawn won every time. 'We all need love,' he added.

'Do we?' Cherry slid out of the car and looked at him. 'Some of us don't seem to . . .' She almost threw the words at him and ran indoors.

He sat still for a while and then started the engine, slowly driving back. A strange evening. It was like a game of Snakes and Ladders. Move forward two . . . ah, on a snake, so back you go six. That was what he had done. He'd seemed to be winning so many times and always ended up by losing more than ever.

158

CHAPTER ELEVEN

When Simon woke on Sunday, his first reaction was pleasure because the sun was shining. A good day to be out in the country with a picnic lunch . . . Then his thoughts crashed to a standstill. They had parted in such a strange mood. Cherry had misunderstood him when he admitted he was jealous, he had meant it as a lead to telling her he loved her and that was the reason for his jealousy, but she had jumped to the conclusion that he was jealous of Shawn because of Aunt Flo!

Oddly enough that had not occurred to him. Though, maybe he thought, turning over in bed and yawning, it was because he had only one thought in his mind: Cherry.

Now what was he to do? Take it for granted that Cherry was so angry with him that if he went to fetch her, she would be even more annoyed. Or treat the whole little scene as if it had never occurred? Should he defend himself and say he didn't begrudge Shawn Aunt Flo's affection? Should he simply tell the truth and say: 'I love you, Cherry Corfield and that is why I am jealous?'

Unable to relax, he got up, showered and dressed, going to stand by the window to look out at the sea. How calm it was, yet it had a threatening gentle swell that promised dangerous currents. It seemed as if that was how his life was at the moment. Whenever he tried to tell Cherry he loved her, they were either interrupted or she mistook what he was saying.

Surely it should be the easiest thing in the world to propose to a girl? Yet somehow it wasn't.

This was what troubled him. Was he subconsciously afraid of marriage? Or afraid of risking a refusal if he did propose? Yet one refusal meant nothing. There were lots of men who went on proposing until they won. What made him hesitate? Why this cautious streak, this feeling of fear lest he speak out of turn or too soon? Who was he afraid of? Himself? Cherry? Or could it be Shawn?

No, that last was ridiculous. His only fear was that Shawn, who had everything Simon wanted and lacked, would win Cherry's love.

He got his own breakfast for, on his off weekends, Mrs. Edwards had a holiday, too. A boiled egg, two pieces of toast, coffee— Simon went through the routine but he tasted nothing. He could only think of the day ahead . . .

If as Betsy said, Cherry liked *him*, why did she keep talking about Shawn? Why did she ask to go to Aunt Flo's, knowing Shawn would be there? She seemed obsessed by Shawn. Surely that meant?

Should he go and fetch her? Or forget the

160

whole thing? He pretended to read and kept glancing at the clock. At eleven-thirty, he stood up. He'd be a fool to miss the chance of being alone with Cherry. There might be a chance, come out of the blue, for him to tell her he loved her.

But there was none. She greeted him as if nothing had happened. He bought a roasted chicken, salad and rolls and butter. They talked casually. Too casually as if both were walking carefully. They talked of Mrs. Chester, of Betsy and Paul, of Cherry's girl friend, Heather, who was in love with a hippie.

'But he's a darling,' Cherry said.

'Why does he look like that?' Simon asked.

'And why shouldn't he look like that?'

'Because they look so . . . well, mucky.'

'He washes his hair every day. Know something, Simon? Although you're only thirty-three, you're an awful square,' Cherry said.

He stared at her. 'Am I?' Perhaps that was the secret? To be 'with it', part of the 'happening'. Was Shawn? Was that his secret?

'What exactly is a square?' he asked coldly.

Cherry, curled up on the rug laid on the cliff high above the still calm sea, looked at him. 'A square is someone who's forgotten he was young once.'

'Oh! Have I?'

'You seem to have. Didn't you do rebellious things? Didn't you ever want to look different

161

. . .'

'But Cherry, that's just it. They don't look different. They all conform, like sheep.'

Cherry jumped up. 'It's useless trying to make you understand. You're so smug in your safe little job with your wonderful house-keeper to wait on you like a slave and your patients to think you're wonderful . . . As I told you in the beginning, you're horribly spoilt.' She walked off back to the car, opened the door and sat down.

What was the good, Simon asked himself, as he hastily collected the remains of their picnic lunch and put them in the basket. He went back to the car and silently slid behind the wheel. He had lost before he started. This was a game in which he could not win and he had better accept it.

Cherry loved Shawn. Shawn!

Yet hope refused to die and as they approached Brighton, Simon's outlook changed again. Why give in when perhaps he had already begun to win? After all, when Cherry saw how Shawn was chatting up the attractive friendly Teresa, it might make her see him with different eyes. If Shawn was the Don Juan that their trip to Amsterdam had made them think he was, then the sooner Cherry realised it the better.

'Nearly there,' he said cheerfully, breaking the long silence.

Cherry looked straight ahead. 'Yes.'

'I wonder if Shawn is here.'

'I wonder,' Cherry said.

Simon had some trouble parking the car and they had to walk along the crowded front before they got to Aunt Flo's.

'I don't know if I'd like to live here,' Simon said, more to break the silence Cherry seemed to be deliberately keeping than anything.

'I've lived in worst places,' she snapped.

Simon was surprised. Now what was wrong? What had he done this time to offend her?

At last they were there! He could hardly wait for the door to open and Cherry start seeing how Shawn could behave. He rang the bell and waited.

The door opened. Teresa stood there. For a moment she just stared and then her face seemed to come to life.

'Simon . . .' she said eagerly. 'Oh, how lovely. We didn't expect you. Do come in. Have you had lunch? I can get you something at once . . .'

She totally ignored Cherry and Simon noticed this with dismay, wondering if Cherry had! It wouldn't help . . .!

'Is Shawn here?' he asked as they went into the narrow hall.

'Shawn? Oh yes, he's with your aunt, Simon. I want to talk to you about your aunt sometime . . .' she said earnestly. She was looking very pretty in white trews and shirt, her hair brushed back, her eyes large and thoughtful.

163

'Alone . . .' she added, giving Cherry her first glance.

Cherry walked by them and opened the door. 'Aunt Flo . . .?' she said, her voice uncertain.

'Later,' Simon said quietly to Teresa. 'I'll come out to the kitchen.'

Teresa smiled. 'I'll be around.'

He went into the room and saw Cherry kissing Aunt Flo. Shawn had been lying on the ground, now he stood up, quickly.

'Simon. My word, it's good to see you,' he said.

'Simon, dear boy,' Aunt Flo beamed and lifted her face for his kiss. 'This is lovely.'

'Cherry's idea,' Simon said and then realised how surly he sounded. 'We had a picnic lunch and thought we'd come and see how you are. And Shawn.' He turned to his brother. 'How're things?'

'I'm just waiting.'

'You'll be glad when it's over.'

Shawn looked rueful. 'You can bet I will.'

'You did tell them about the concussion?'

Rubbing his hand wearily over his face, Shawn said: 'I'm sure I did. I told them everything. They asked the same questions over and over again. I'd hate to be lying for I'm sure I'd be tripped up.'

Simon grinned. 'I imagine that's the idea.'

Shawn nodded. 'I can imagine. Look . . .' he smiled at them all. 'Let's take Aunt Flo out for a drive and have tea somewhere.'

'That would be delightful,' Aunt Flo said. 'Can I go with you, Shawn?'

Simon stared at her. So though Aunt Flo would not go with *him*, if she could help it, she was willing to go with Shawn, who'd had car accidents whereas Simon had never . . . well, actually he hadn't had an accident that was his fault. But then, he remembered, neither had it been *Shawn's* fault that the trailer had gone sliding down the hill, crushing every car on its way.

'I'll come with you,' Cherry said eagerly. 'Simon can bring Teresa.'

Teresa came into the room, smiling. 'Did I hear my name?'

They told her and she thought it was a lovely idea. Later as Simon drove them, a comfortable distance behind Shawn's sports car, apparently hired for his visit to Brighton, Teresa said:

'I'm worried about your aunt.'

'Why, is she ill?'

Teresa shook her head. 'Not at all but . . . Look, Simon, I'm not sure it's a good idea. My looking after her, I mean. She's doing less and less and sitting more and more at the window, just staring at the buses and people.'

'You mean she's given up . . . ?'

'Yes. We're making her feel old and helpless.'

'But she said you were a comfort and . . .'

'That was because you're paying me a salary and she didn't want you to feel she didn't like me around all the time. She does like me to pop in for a visit but she also likes to be allowed to do her own work, shopping and everything. As it is, she is bored to death . . .' Her hand flew to her mouth but her eyes were grave as she nodded. 'Maybe I used the right word, after all. If she goes on sitting there doing nothing, she'll get fat and so bored that . . . well, she'll just give in.'

Simon slowed up as the lights changed to red. Shawn had got through and was going far ahead.

'So what d'you suggest?' he asked.

'You sack me.' Teresa laughed. 'I want to be sacked Simon, please. That's why I was so pleased to see you this afternoon. I've been planning a letter but it's much better to say these things.'

'You want to go?'

'M'm. Shawn has been telling me all about Australia and it sounds pretty great. A school friend of mine and I are thinking of emigrating. I feel I'd be happier right away from here with all its memories. Start a new life . . . That's why I wanted to see you. I don't want you to think I'm dropping Aunt Flo. I won't be going for some time but I suggest we go back into the old role. I'll pop in now and then but get a job so that she knows she's got to cope.'

'But can she?'

'When she has to and she loves it.'

'But she's not far off eighty and . . .'

'Simon. I've known women of eighty-seven who live alone and do everything. They say that's how they stay well and happy. The trouble is, you know, so often we, with the best intentions, practically kill our old people. They don't want too much cossetting and fussing. They want to be treated like normal human beings not like old senile invalids.'

He laughed. 'You could be right. I had a patient who was just like that. She hated her age being mentioned and got really mad if anyone sympathised with her.'

'Well, what shall we do?'

'Better do it gently,' he said. 'Talk of getting a job, let her do some of the things you've been doing . . . or if you prefer it, talk frankly with her. Tell her I won't be hurt. I only want her to be happy.'

Now he had caught up with the red sports car. Shawn waved and they turned off the main road. Obviously Aunt Flo was guiding them to one of her favourite tea rooms. Until a few years earlier, Aunt Flo had had her own car. It was only when she had some bouts of dizziness that she had decided to sell it. Now Simon wondered if it was his insistence that she was a menace to others as well as herself, that had persuaded her, and was she now regretting it?

He sighed as he parked the car and they

went inside the shop. It seemed that these days, he could never win!

It was much, much later that evening that Simon made his big mistake. After tea, they had driven round the lovely countryside, showing Shawn what rural England was like, and then went back to Aunt Flo's flat. Teresa deftly produced a casserole and found bananas and raisins she mashed together, and a good evening meal was eaten by the five of them. It was as they drank their farewell cup of coffee that Shawn said suddenly:

'Genetics are queer things, aren't they, Simon? It intrigues me how we inherit different tendencies and how, as we grow older, we change. It's odd when we come to think of it that you were the little runt, the delicate child, always wheezing with bronchitis or asthma or something. I was the tough one. Yet now we're grown up, you are the strong heathy one while I'm in and out of hospitals ...'

Later Simon, going over the scene, realised that this was the last straw. He'd had Shawn, Shawn, Shawn all day. Aunt Flo had glowed loving at him, encouraging him to talk. Cherry had listened to his stories of life in the outback, Teresa thinking of emigrating to that wonderland, had also sat, entranced. Simon had felt left out. Completely and utterly left out. Shawn had walked into his life and taken his place. Maybe that was why Simon made such an unfortunate statement, a statement he was to regret the more he thought of it.

'Maybe you'd stay out of hospital,' Simon had said, 'if you stopped driving sports cars.'

Even before he saw the quick pain on Shawn's face, Simon regretted the words. Aunt Flo caught her breath and looked horrified. Cherry stared at him as if she hated him for his cruelty.

Teresa, perhaps unconsciously, stepped into the breach, so to speak.

'It must be terrible fun racing. Aren't you frightfully squashed in? And with all those clothes and that helmet . . .'

Shawn had quickly recovered. 'Actually, I don't race, Teresa, though many of my friends do.'

Driving Cherry home, they hardly spoke. He walked with her to the door of her flat.

'Goodnight,' she said coldly.

That morning he had planned that, after a day together, talking, relaxing, maybe he'd find the courage that night to break his silence and tell her he loved her. He was sure *he* did, but he could not know how she felt until he asked her.

But now he knew it was no good. She would never forgive him for that stupid cruel remark.

CHAPTER TWELVE

The next morning, immediately after breakfast, Simon phoned his brother.

'I'm sorry about that stupid remark,' Simon said bluntly.

Shawn gave a half-laugh. 'I know. I saw that at once. Don't worry, Simon. I know you didn't mean it. So often these things shouldn't be said yet we get landed with them.'

'Well, thanks, I felt very bad. Look, Shawn, we've never really had the chance to know one another. How about coming over and staying with me for a couple of days? I can borrow a spare camp bed.'

'I'd like that, my word I would,' Shawn said. 'I feel it's all wrong that though we're twins, we're so far apart. I gather from Aunt Flo, though, that you're often on call in the evenings?'

'I can get that fixed so that we have several evenings free.'

'That'ud be great. Let me know which days.'

'Okay. Shawn. I'll talk to the others today and see what I can arrange,' Simon said and rang off.

He had no difficulty in arranging free evenings and four days later, Shawn arrived. The first evening they sat and talked about pretty nearly everything. Finally got to religion and politics and found they both took the same point of view. They talked about girls and here there was a difference, Simon saw marriage as a serious matter but to Shawn, it was a waste of time.

'What's the good of a scrap of paper that says you're wed?' he asked. 'You can be a hypocrite and have a lover and still be called a good Christian because you're wed.'

'All the same, the kids . . .' Simon said.

Shawn nodded. 'I agree with you all the way, there. Thing is, don't have kids unless you are absolutely sure you're right for one another.'

Simon sighed. 'How can you be sure?'

Grinning, Shawn shrugged. 'Big question of the day. How, indeed! This Dutch girl. I thought I was crazy about her. Then she began to talk of marriage, the sort of house she'd like, how many children and I felt I was being caught in a trap. Apart from that, I don't think I should marry until . . .' He paused, looking thoughtfully at Simon. 'Why haven't *you* married, anyhow?'

'I thought I was going to marry once. Five years ago. She married someone else. Apparently the thought of being a doctor's wife didn't appeal.'

'Five years is a long time.'

Simon smiled. 'A broken heart takes a long time to heal.'

'It's healed now?'

'Sure.' He felt like adding that it was about

to be broken again, but decided not to.

'You'd like to be married? You don't mind all those ties and responsibilities? I mean, of marriage?'

'I never thought of it in that way,' Simon admitted. 'I loved the girl and wanted her to be mine.'

'And now?'

Simon hesitated. Should he tell Shawn the truth? Or was that fair? If Shawn and Cherry were in love . . .

Fortunately the phone bell shrilled so he escaped having to answer. It was Betsy!

'I hear that brother of yours is with you. Can you both come to dinner tomorrow night, Simon? We're having some young couples and then going on to the Cinderella Dance afterwards. You know it. In aid of charity and Paul and I always support it though I'm not sure what charity it is this year.'

'Well, I . . . we . . .' Simon began.

Shawn looked at him with questions in his eyes so Simon put his hand over the phone and whispered. 'Asked out to dinner and then a dance? Appeal to you?'

'I'm easy. Sounds fun,' Shawn said.

Betsy spoke impatiently. 'Do stop muttering, Simon. Of course you're coming, both of you. I've already asked Cherry and another girl so it should be quite nice.'

'All right,' Simon said and, rather belatedly, added: 'Thanks.' He put down the receiver.

172

Cherry would be there! Was she on speaking terms with him, he wondered.

The next day was a busy one for Simon. There was a slight epidemic of gastroenteritis and one of the doctors was off, so Simon had little or no time to worry about Shawn. That evening as he showered and changed into a dark suit, he asked his brother how he'd spent the day.

'Hope you weren't too bored. Afraid I can't be very sociable.'

Shawn was having a last minute shave though, with his fair hair, he hardly needed to do so. 'That's okay, Simon. I had a great day. Rang Cherry and we went to Rye and all round. I enjoyed it . . .'

'I bet you did . . .' Simon said silently as he combed his hair before the mirror. He might have known that would happen so it had been stupid to ask.

The dinner party was a great success. At least for everyone but himself, Simon thought. Cherry *was* speaking to him but there was that look of hatred in her eyes again, the look she'd had that first day he'd noticed her. The other young couples were gay and amusing. A girl called Anastasia Johnson, younger than Cherry and a glamorous-looking model, was the *spare* girl. She kept joking and laughing, saying she never knew if she was talking to Shawn or Simon.

'It could be quite complicating,' she joked.

173

'I can tell,' Cherry said. 'Easily . . .' and she looked at Simon coldly.

'I'm sure we're quite different,' Simon said quickly.

Cherry smiled. A cold unfriendly smile. 'Quite different,' she agreed.

Later they went to the dance. Simon saw immediately that Shawn was a much better dancer than he was. He danced twice with Cherry and found himself constantly treading on her feet and apologising. Something that had not happened in Amsterdam when they danced. Later he danced with Anastasia who teased him, saying it was like dancing with an elephant and why didn't he have lessons.

'I don't often dance,' he confessed, shouting above the noise of laughter, voices and music.

'Why not? Even a doctor can't work all day,' Anastasia told him. She had long narrow eyes with incredible lashes, a full pouting mouth, beautiful creamy skin, and dark hair piled high on her head. 'I can see I must take you under my wing,' she added.

'You don't live here, do you?' Simon asked.

'No but I often come down weekends. We'll fix something,' Anastasia smiled at him.

There was a press photographer from the local paper and photos were taken. But the photographer must have got a little confused for several days later when the local paper came out, there was a picture of Cherry in Shawn's arms, gazing soulfully up in his eyes

174

and the caption said: 'Dr. Britten may be interested in romance after all.'

Shawn had gone back to Brighton, Simon stared at the photo. Cherry *must* be in love with Shawn, surely? Otherwise why was she gazing at him like that?

Later she phoned him. 'I'm afraid the reporter mixed you up,' she said apologetically. 'I told him that it was Shawn. I hope you don't mind? I mean . . .'

'Why should I mind?'

'I thought you didn't like being teased.'

'I don't mind. I don't mind at all.'

'So it doesn't matter? I'm glad,' Cherry said and put down the receiver. Simon stood still for a moment, not sure if it had been a friendly conversation or an antagonistic one.

Ah well, he sighed, it had been a wonderful dream while it lasted. Pity was it might have lasted longer if Shawn hadn't turned up!

Of course he didn't mind, about the photo, Simon told himself. Not really. All the same, it was going to be embarrassing, for his patients loved to tease him about his bachelorhood state. In any case it meant publicity and that was something every doctor avoided.

However it turned out better than he had feared. Apparently very few people bothered to read the small captions below the photographs and took it for granted that Simon had just gone to a dance and had his photo taken! The gastroenteritis problem grew bigger and the days flew by with Simon taking little notice of the time or even thinking of Cherry.

So it was a real surprise when she phoned him.

'Simon—isn't tomorrow the day Shawn has to appear in court?'

'Is it? I don't know. I can't remember,' Simon was confused, surprised by her phoning him, annoyed that it must always be something to do with Shawn. 'Why? He'll know.'

'But he isn't there,' she said and sounded desperate.

'He . . . he isn't there? You mean Brighton?'

'No. Yes . . . I mean no he isn't there and yes I mean Brighton,' Cherry said impatiently. 'I happened to ring Aunt Flo this morning . . .'

Happened! Simon thought bitterly. A likely story. He supposed Cherry wanted to contact Shawn and thought it more tactful to do it through his aunt.

'She said she hadn't seen him for two days and was a little worried. I said what about ringing the hotel and she said she hadn't liked to do that as she didn't want him to think she was possessive. So I said I would . . .'

'I see . . .' Simon murmured. So Cherry didn't mind being thought possessive? And she must be equally sure that Shawn wouldn't see it as possessive, either!

'Well, Simon, Shawn's gone. Vanished.'

'Look, Cherry, calm down. You do

176

dramatise so. What d'you mean by the word *vanished*? Has he left the hotel, paid his bill, etc. perhaps left a forwarding address?'

'None of those things. He hasn't paid his bill or taken his clothes. They're still in his room. Apparently he hasn't been seen since yesterday. Simon, I'm frightened for him. Could he have been in an accident and gone into hospital . . .'

'They would have found some means of identifying him. Perhaps he got bored and just went away for a few days.'

'They said he hadn't even taken a toothbrush.'

'Oh. Well, look, Shawn isn't a child. I don't think we need flap like mad . . .'

'How can you be so callous. He is your brother,' Cherry said angrily.

'I just don't like interfering.'

'Interfering! He may need help . . .' Cherry almost shouted.

It was as if something rang a bell in Simon's head. Shawn needing help . . .?

The police would have something to say if he didn't turn up. And there was that curious something about Shawn that had puzzled Simon, something he could not discover without Shawn being frank and having a complete medical examination. Could Shawn be suffering from temporary amnesia? Or a blackout?'

'You know you're right, Cherry,' Simon's

voice changed. 'He may need help. Look, don't worry but leave it to me. I'll contact the police and tell them what I'm afraid of . . .'

'What you're afraid of? I don't understand, Simon.'

'Well, I'm not sure, you see. I have a feeling that . . . well, that Shawn isn't a hundred per cent fit. It could be affecting him in some way or another. Amnesia . . .'

'What's that?'

'Loss of memory.' Simon thought fast. 'I must deal with the police first. I think I'll go up to town right away and see those concerned. Meanwhile Cherry, if you don't mind, would you ring the different hospitals in Brighton to see if an unknown man is there. I was thinking, he might only have his Australian papers on him and no means of getting in touch with Aunt Flo or me.'

'I'll do that, Simon,' Cherry promised. 'Thanks . . .'

Simon rang up and phoned Paul Donward. What had she thanked him for, he wondered.

'Paul, Shawn's in some kind of trouble and . . .'

Paul sighed dramatically. 'Not again! My poor Simon. you must curse the day that brother of yours turned up. Serious?'

'I don't know.' Briefly Simon described his intuition about Shawn. 'I haven't asked him but he did say an odd thing the other day. That I was the delicate child and healthy as can be

178

now whereas he was the tough child and the reverse now. I didn't think of it at the time but . . .'

'So he's just vanished?'

'Yes. Left everything behind, including his toothbrush.' Simon managed a laugh. 'Cherry seems to think that is conclusive evidence that he had no intention of going. He has to appear in Court tomorrow so I've got to rush to London and cope with the police.'

'And Shawn?'

'Cherry's phoning the Brighton hospitals for me . . .'

'It could have happened anywhere . . .'

'I know. Will it be all right if I take off right away?'

'Of course, Simon. I'll fix things. I hope . . . look, if there's anything I can do?'

'Thanks Paul.' Simon hesitated. 'Cherry is rather hysterical. I don't know what she fears but I imagine it is the worst. Perhaps Betsy . . .?'

'Sure. I'll get on to her right away. See you sometime, then.'

'Thanks.'

Simon hastily packed an overnight bag in case the police proved difficult, then rushed to the station. As he settled back in the train, he remembered Paul's words:

'You must curse the day that brother of yours turned up.'

Oddly enough, Simon thought, he didn't. He might have done a few days ago but somehow he had accepted the fact that he had lost the girl he loved to his brother. After all, it wasn't Shawn's fault. It was his.

That first day when Shawn said:

'Is she yours?'

Simon knew he should have said firmly 'Yes'. Had he done that, Shawn would have left her alone.

It was easy to be wise when the damage is done, he told himself, and unfolded the *Evening News.* He read without taking in what he was reading but anything was better than sitting here, thinking, wondering, knowing how anything that happened to Shawn would hurt Cherry.

CHAPTER THIRTEEN

It was not quite as simple as Simon had expected and he found himself shuffled from one man to another, even from one station to finally Scotland Yard. What annoyed him was the way they would say: 'Mr. Shawn Britten . . .'

And he would reply. 'No. I am Dr. Simon Britten. Shawn is my twin brother,' and they would smile!

He knew they did not believe him. When finally he was taken to the office of a very pleasant grey-haired man whose eyes were amused and whose mouth kept curving in a smile, Simon began to wonder how he would ever convince them.

'Mr. Shawn Britten. You were requested to contact us this morning.'

'I am not Shawn Britten,' Simon said for what seemed like the hundredth time. 'I am his twin brother, Dr. Simon Britten . . .'

It was like hearing an old record with the needle stuck in the same place, repeating the words until you wanted to scream. 'I've come because he's disappeared. When I say that,' Simon added hastily, 'I don't mean deliberately. I am afraid he is ill.'

Luke Grant looked serious for a moment. 'What makes you say that?'

Simon described as quickly as he could small actions Shawn made, uncontrollable jerks of the elbow, a sudden blank look. an inability to answer a simple question. 'It's impossible to be sure without a proper examination, of course.'

'You must admit it is very convenient for him to have an attack at this time,' Luke Grant pointed out.

'Look . . .' Simon drew a deep breath. 'Emotional trouble could trigger it off. Shawn was furious with himself for having been such a fool . . .'

'He does admit he did it? I mean, he's not thought of accusing you?'

'Of course not. He's not like that.'

'How long have you known him?'

Simon's temper was rising. 'Long enough. Shawn knew he'd been a fool and could have caused a tragedy. He's been staying in Brighton where our Aunt Flo lives. She brought me up,' he explained. 'Then he vanished. The hotel says he hasn't taken any clothes or . . . well, or anything. Not even his toothbrush.'

'It could be to make you think he was ill.'

'It could be, I suppose,' Simon sighed. 'Look, Shawn isn't like that. He may be a coward, aren't we all, but he wouldn't run away like this. What's the point? He could always be caught with his Australian passport to give him away. No. I'm afraid he's had an attack of amnesia—often brought on by a traumatic experience, and this could be called one—and is lying in some hospital.'

'Have you any idea if he has his passport with him? I was thinking that if he had, we could trace him more easily.'

'I have no idea. I didn't go to the hotel. When I was told he wasn't there and had just vanished I came straight up here to see if we could postpone the hearing. I didn't want you to think . . .'

Luke Grant put his fingers together thoughtfully. 'Look, just tell me the whole story, from the day you were born. Keep it as brief as you can—only it seems to me a most peculiar relationship. Not unnaturally we are inclined to believe it a big bluff . . .'

'All right.' Simon spoke, thinking fast as he did, discarding what was unnecessary, emphasizing what was necessary. He told Luke Grant of his delicate childhood, the father taking the healthy child, the long silence.

'I had no idea I had a twin brother. I had the shock of my life when I met him. It was like staring in a mirror at your own reflection. Most people find it difficult to distinguish us, too, which can be rather embarrassing.'

'And why do you think he has this . . . well, this illness?'

'He's been involved in several car accidents. Had concussion. Also he is emotionally unstable. An unhappy love-starved childhood and suddenly he has a twin brother and an aunt who loves him like a mother. These things sound trivial, I know, but they can add up especially if he has this . . . well, let's face it. I'm only guessing. I've no evidence. Just a feeling.'

Luke Grant grinned. 'Psychic?' he asked. He stood up. 'There's someone I'd like you to see. Just wait a moment.'

Simon nodded. 'Mind if I smoke?'

'Of course not. There is an ashtray.' Luke Grant left the room, closing the door gently.

Slowly Simon lit the cigarette and glanced round the square white-walled room. Luke Grant was being patient but somehow Simon felt sure that he didn't believe a word of what he had heard.

The door opened and Simon looked up. Instantly he was on his feet. A tall beautiful blonde haired girl stood there, staring at him.

'Shawn my darling. It is I who have been unhappy for you. When they said you weren't . . .' the girl said rushing at Simon, flinging her arms round him, kissing him on the mouth.

And then she stood back, her face changing. her hands falling to her sides. 'You're not Shawn,' she said. 'You must be the other one.'

'The other one,' Luke Grant prompted gently.

Madeleine Zykmayer turned to him. 'Yes, this one is he whose face I smacked . . .' She half smiled, turning to Simon. 'I owe you an apology but you are so alike.'

'You're certain this isn't Shawn Britten?' Luke Grant asked.

'Quite certain. He is so different.'

'But you just said they were so alike,' Luke Grant sounded bewildered.

Madeleine laughed. 'To look at, yes. But kissing. Ah no, he is very different from my Shawn. It was like kissing a stone. Even if he did not know her, when a pretty girl kisses Shawn, he reacts . . .' She laughed at the look on Luke Grant's face. 'Is that not so? Some men react instantly. Others, they are so slow. But not my Shawn. He is the fast one.'

'You were saying, Miss Zykmayer, that you were worried about Shawn Britten's health. Dr. Britten has expressed the same fear.'

Madeleine turned eagerly to Simon, holding out her hands. 'You agree? My Shawn, he worries me. He will not tell me a thing. He told you?'

'Nothing. Nothing at all. It was just the way he behaves, odd things he has said. I've seen very little of him and it's difficult to tell a man you've just met that he should go for a medical check-up.'

'It is serious,' she told him, 'But need not be. I wondered sometimes, also, about Shawn. Two bad car accidents and then . . . well, he was never the same. He told me nothing—but nothing at all. So I had him followed.' She shrugged. 'Maybe I shouldn't but I love him. I learned he was going regularly to a specialist. So, when he came over here to meet you, Dr. Britten, I went to the specialist. He gave me long words I can't remember but he says that Shawn must take to bed for six months or else there may be real trouble.'

'That's what I was afraid of. How is it you're here?'

Somehow both had forgotten Luke Grant, standing quietly in the background. He made no attempt to attract their attention, perhaps he preferred it this way, he might have thought he'd hear more.

'I have my friends in England. They told me about the stupid hoax and when the case would be heard so I arranged to be here, to be with my Shawn and to tell him that he was a

185

fool but I knew he meant no harm. And you, why are you here and not Shawn?'

Simon told her briefly. She looked worried.

'But he might be anywhere. Dead . . . in hospital or just walking round. Is nothing being done to find him?'

Luke Grant spoke then. 'We are making every effort to find him, Miss Zykmayer. You are going to marry Mr. Britten?'

'Most certainly.' The girl looked shocked. 'He has told you, of course?' she turned to Simon.

He shook his head, remembering all that Shawn had said of this girl.

'He said nothing about marriage but then,' he added, sorry for her hurt look, 'we have had little time to talk.'

'Ah . . .' She smiled. 'There were other things that must be discussed. Am I right?' She laughed. 'How amusing to find you have a twin brother. D'you think alike?'

'About most things.'

Luke Grant coughed a little so they turned to him.

'You are staying in London, Miss Zykmayer?'

'But of course. I hope to take my Shawn home with me.' She looked pathetic and very lovely. 'That is, if your people are understanding. Shawn must have been ill. Always he likes the joke but never if there is violence.' She shook her head, her beautiful blonde hair shining. 'No, that is not my Shawn.'

'And you Dr. Britten?' Luke Grant asked.

Simon hesitated. 'I came prepared to stay but I'm wondering if I oughtn't to go down to Brighton. You see, Shawn has hired a car but I don't know the number or the firm he hired it from but my Aunt Flo might. Then if we have the number, it would be easier to trace it if there was an accident.'

'True.' Luke Grant looked thoughtful. 'What was the car? The colour? You've seen it?'

'Yes, a red sports car. I don't know what make.'

'Please stay in London. That is if you can . . .' Madeleine said, putting her hand on his sleeve. 'I am so lonely. If I can talk to you, it will not be so painful.'

'I think I'd prefer it,' Luke Grant said. 'We can get in touch with the garages in Brighton—he did hire it there?'

'Yes. I'm almost sure he did. He said he'd rather get used to our traffic signs and things in Brighton than in London. I remember that.'

'Thank you. May I have your aunt's address? I think we should see her. She might be able to give us some clue. However small, it could be useful.'

'I don't know if I can get a hotel. It's summer . . .' Simon said.

'We try my hotel,' Madeleine smiled.

187

'Always we stay there. It is expensive but good. They will wish to please me, I am certain.'

So they parted with Luke Grant, who made a note of the hotel and promised to ring them if any discovery was made. He assured Simon that there was no need to worry about the Court. Something could be arranged.

It was, or rather would have been, a pleasant evening if Simon could have stopped worrying about Shawn. Madeleine bravely put on a gay face, though occasionally she would be dismal and appear to weep but Simon grew rather sceptical. Did this girl really love Shawn? He had thought so to begin with but as the evening passed, he began to doubt.

She sulked when he said he must make a few phone calls.

'You leave me alone when I am so sad?'

'I will be as quick as I can.'

He had kept his word. Telling Paul briefly what had happened.

'Simon, Cherry is here and longing to speak to you,' Paul said.

'Is she?'

Cherry spoke. 'How did you get on, Simon? Were they beastly to you?'

'Not at all. The reverse though I think they still believe I am bluffing and that I am really Shawn Britten.'

'But Simon, surely you can prove . . .'

'Maybe I have. The Dutch girl is here and . . .' Simon began and stopped dead, shocked at what he had said. He had not intended to mention Madeleine, for he was sure Shawn wasn't in love with the Dutch girl and there was no point in making Cherry wonder and be unhappy about the unknown girl.

'Dutch girl?' Cherry repeated and laughed. 'Oh, yes, the one who planned their lives and Shawn ran fast to get away.'

Simon relaxed. 'You know? Oh well. She turned up very upset. Thought I was Shawn, flung herself at me and then said it wasn't Shawn.'

'She knew the difference?'

'She said I didn't kiss properly . . .' Simon said and wondered why he had.

'Kiss properly?' Cherry sounded puzzled. 'Why did you kiss her?'

'I didn't. That was it. She kissed me and, so she says, I didn't respond.'

'But Shawn would. Is that what she said?' Cherry asked.

Simon drew a deep breath. He really was putting his foot in it. 'Well, of course he would, because he was in love with her at one stage,' Simon said quickly.

Cherry laughed. 'That wasn't what she meant. Simon, what's happening? Where are you?'

'Madeleine wanted me to stay in London. She said she was lonely and afraid.'

'I see. She must be very lovely.'

'Oh, she is. A model, long slim legs,

189

gorgeous hair . . .'

'And the police?'

'They thought it best for me to be around. They're searching for Shawn. We're rather afraid he may have amnesia.'

'We?' Cherry repeated, her voice odd.

'Madeleine and I are. She saw Shawn's specialist and he says Shawn must have complete rest in bed for six months or . . .' Simon stopped abruptly. Why was he telling poor Cherry all this? It could only upset her.

'Or . . .?' Cherry echoed.

He fidgeted. 'Well, it could be serious, Cherry, but I'm sure when we make Shawn understand, he'll have the sense to take his doctor's advice. I must go, Cherry. I want to ring Aunt Flo. The police are going to question her.'

'Oh no,' Cherry almost wailed. 'But why?'

'Nothing unpleasant. Just details about the car he hired and when she last saw him. Don't worry, Cherry, they'll be gentle with her. And I'm sure Shawn will be all right. 'Bye.'

He rang off then rang Aunt Flo.

She was glad he was doing something constructive.

'Teresa has been ringing all the hospitals but so far we have nothing, nothing at all. The police? Of course, dear boy, if I can do anything to help. He was rather quiet, I thought. As if he was thinking seriously about something. Well, yes, I suppose in a way I

190

would say he was different.'

'Yes, I'm afraid he's not well, Aunt Flo. Nothing serious but he was obviously troubled about the whole affair and I'm afraid he may have amnesia but it isn't serious, Aunt Flo. Don't worry and I'll phone you tomorrow.'

'Yes, dear boy. I'll look forward to it.'

Simon went back slowly to Madeleine. She hadn't missed him! There was a couple at her table, drinking coffee with her, and a tall thin man with a small pointed black beard.

'Ah Simon . . .' she said and introduced him all round. 'My future brother-in-law . . .' she said and smiled.

Simon excused himself as soon as he could and went to his bedroom. He didn't feel sleepy. He stood by the window gazing at the lights of London and the traffic. He wondered how Cherry was feeling. Poor Cherry. If only . . .

CHAPTER FOURTEEN

Simon was finishing his breakfast when he was paged. He read the note he was given. It was written in big flowery handwriting.

'Simon, my dear future brother-in-law. I have friends here to see me at ten o'clock. Could you come and meet them? It would make it easier for me. Do not answer. I know I can rely on you.'

191

It was signed with a flourishing: Madeleine.

Sighing a little, Simon folded the letter and put it away. He could not forget that Madeleine meant more trouble ahead for Cherry. When they found Shawn, which would be his choice? Madeleine or Cherry?

Simon went to the phone and called Luke Grant.

'No news yet, I'm afraid.'

'Look, must I stay up here?' Simon asked worriedly. 'I feel so utterly useless.'

Luke Grant laughed. 'There's no *must* about it. Simply I would prefer you to be on hand when we find your brother.'

'I'd rather be out looking for him but . . . I've got to meet some of Madeleine Zykmayer's relatives at ten this morning, then I'll come along. I can't just sit here.'

'You seem well under the thumb of your future sister-in-law,' Luke Grant's voice was dry.

'Quite frankly, I don't think she will ever be my sister-in-law. I know Shawn was . . . well, in his own words, crazy about her but her possessive bossiness scared him. I'm beginning to see what he means.'

Luke Grant chuckled. 'I'm not surprised. Look, who your brother marries is his cup of tea and I'm busy. 'Bye.'

' 'Bye . . .' Simon put down the receiver slowly. Shawn's *cup of tea*? Surely Cherry's as well? If once again, she was to be hurt . . . If only, Simon thought desperately, he could do something to help.

At ten o'clock, he made his way to Madeleine's suite; Her father must be extremely wealthy, Simon thought, as he went in the luxuriously furnished room, with golden silk curtains and white carpet, bowls of flowers everywhere and . . .

He stopped dead in the doorway, his face shocked. As he turned to go out, Madeleine came running, catching his arm, sliding between him and the door.

'Darling, I was afraid you would not come. You have been to the police . . . ?'

Simon could not speak for a moment as he stared at the brilliant lights, the cameras, the men and girls with their notebooks ready.

'What is this?' he asked. 'A press conference?'

Madeleine squeezed his arm. 'Of course. What else is it possible it could be?' She laughed. 'You have seen the daily paper? No? Why not? This is the way to find Shawn. My photo was in it. If he sees it, he will remember everything . . .'

'Madeleine. I must go.' Simon tried to free his arm but her fingers clung to it. He looked round the crowded room rather wildly. Short of being brutal, what could he do? 'I don't want this sort of publicity . . .'

She pouted. 'But it is only to help your brother, Simon.'

A short, plumpish man with curly red hair came forward.

'We appreciate your dislike of publicity, Dr. Britten,' he said gently. 'But it could help to trace your missing twin brother, you know. Is it true you had no idea until recently that you had a brother? Surely this was a little odd? You had been adopted?'

Simon hesitated but what harm could there be in answering these sort of questions. 'Actually what happened was . . .'

'Come and sit down,' the red-headed man said with a friendly smile. Simon sat on the peach-coloured couch, Madeleine by his side, and he answered the questions.

About Aunt Flo, the delicate child, the father taking the strong one . . . 'I undersand from Miss Zykmayer that your brother is now the delicate one?'

'So I gather. I have an idea he might be suffering from amnesia, or some kind of delayed shock could cause a blackout.'

'It must have been embarrassing to find someone who looked exactly like you.'

'It was,' Simon laughed.

'I knew he wasn't Shawn,' Madeleine said. 'As soon as I kissed him.'

There was a ripple of quickly suppressed mirth. Simon's cheeks were hot.

'He doesn't kiss like his brother?' the red-haired man sounded amused.

Madeleine laughed, moved her long white

194

fingers expressively. 'No two men kiss alike. I should know . . .' she said, looking round her. 'Every woman knows. But Shawn, he kisses so . . . how shall I express myself? So warmly, so excitingly . . .' She hugged herself and smiled. 'Simon! He didn't even kiss me. It was like kissing a stone . . .'

Simon's face went even more red as the interviewer looked at him with lifted eyebrows and a twisted mouth as if he was trying not to laugh.

'You don't like kissing girls, Br. Britten?'

'I only kiss the girls I love . . . Look, this is quite absurd and has nothing to do with finding my brother. If this is all we're going to talk about . . .' Simon began to stand up, but Madeleine jerked at his arm.

'He is very sensitive, this one. So easy to hurt. Not like my Shawn. He bounces back,' she said.

'Dr. Britten. I appreciate your feelings and apologise. You have no idea where your brother could be at this moment?'

'Of course not. If I had, I wouldn't be sitting here.'

'Exactly. You have the police looking?'

Simon sighed. 'If you'll excuse me, I said I'd go along to help them. I'm seriously worried about my brother and am wasting my time sitting here.'

Madeleine pouted. 'I think this may find him.'

'I hope so.' Simon stood up. 'If you'll excuse me. I'll see you later, Madeleine.'

'Yes and if you have news, you will tell me?'

'Of course. Immediately.'

At last, Simon managed to get outside the room. Whew . . . he thought. He could imagine Betsy's mirth and Paul's jokes when they saw him on television. He had forgotten to ask which channel. Not that he was interested.

He went to his room, packed his overnight case and went down to the reception desk, paying his account and then making a phone call to Paul.

'They seem to want me to hang around but I could get anywhere just as fast from Hastings as from up here,' Simon said impatiently. 'I'm going mad with nothing to do.'

Paul chuckled. 'I'd have thought you'd plenty to do with that beautiful girl.'

'Spare me the jokes,' Simon almost groaned. 'I'll never live this down. You may see me on the telly tonight.'

'No?' Paul shouted. 'Wait till I tell Betsy. We shall sit glued to that little box, my lad. I wonder what you'll look like.'

'Ghastly I expect for I was in a filthy temper. She tricked me into it. You know darned well that had I known the cameras were there, nothing would have induced me to go to her suite.'

'Suite.' Paul whistled. 'Looks as if your brother is on to a good thing.'

'I wonder. She's possessive and bossy and . . .'

'Wealthy,' Paul provided. 'A man can forgive a lot for that.'

Simon hesitated. 'Is Cherry around . . . I mean, have you seen her?'

'No, she went over to Brighton to see your aunt. She seemed to think your aunt might remember something your brother had said that might be a clue.'

'I see.' Simon paused again. 'I expect she's very worried.'

'Who? Your aunt?' Paul asked. 'Yes, I gathered that from what Cherry said. It's normal, isn't it. This girl of his. Is she really in love with him or is it all a show?'

'I don't know. I honestly don't. Heaven help poor Shawn if he marries her, though. I'd run so fast . . .'

Paul chuckled. '*You* run away, anyhow, as soon as marriage is mentioned. Seriously, though, Simon. I'd be glad if you could gently twist the police's arm and come back. I'll guarantee you if necessary. Only we're short-handed. Pierce is down with some weird bug we can't trace at the moment, and . . . well, frankly, things are a bit chaotic.'

'I'm going along to Scotland Yard now. I'm sure they'll say it's okay. They said I hadn't *got* to stay, anyhow.'

After a few more moments chatter, they rang off and Simon, taking his overnight bag with him, hurried to see Luke Grant. Anything would be better than this hanging about . . . and as Paul needed him . . .

When Simon finally saw Luke Grant, the tall grey-haired man nodded. 'Of course, Dr. Britten. By all means, go.'

Simon thanked him and the telephone bell shrilled.

'Just a moment,' Luke Grant said, and answered it. He listened silently, rarely speaking. 'I see . . . She did? . . . You had . . . I'd like to speak to her.'

He put his hand over the receiver and looked at Simon.

'Your brother's girl friend . . .'

Then he spoke into the phone. 'Yes, please tell me everything. I understand . . . No, you did quite right. Yes, thanks. I see . . .'

The one-sided conversation told Simon nothing. He wondered what on earth Madeleine could have discovered since he last saw her.

When Luke Grant was finished, he pushed the telephone aside and looked at Simon.

'Your brother is in hospital at St. Ives, Cornwall. He was found unconscious in his car early this morning . . .'

'Cornwall?' Simon leant forward. 'He's all right?'

'Still unconscious, apparently. He must have stopped abruptly just inches off a drop over the cliff. There were skidding marks as if he tried to stop earlier. He must have hit his head on the steering wheel, they think, for it went into a tree. Would you think it was attempted suicide?'

'Most certainly not,' Simon said quickly. 'Shawn isn't like that. But what was he doing in Cornwall?'

'It seems his parents met there and he wanted to see the place. Your Aunt Flo when talking to us, said she vaguely remembered having said something about the past to your brother but couldn't recall it. Now your brother's girl friend tells me she remembered his talking about Carbis Bay so she went there. If she hadn't, he might have been there indefinitely. It is, apparently, very overgrown and is a well-known danger spot so few people ever go there.'

'When did she find him? I mean, she's still in London . . .' Simon felt confused as well as relieved. 'How . . .'

'I don't mean Miss Zykmayer. A Miss Corfield phoned me.'

'Cherry . . .' Simon nodded. 'I didn't even know she'd gone down to Cornwall.'

'You've been up here,' Luke Grant pointed out. 'Look, we'll be getting a medical report and when your brother is well, we'll look into the other matter. Not to worry just now. First thing is to get him back to normal health . . .'

If they ever could, Simon thought, as he hurried to the nearest public call box. Why on earth had the car skidded? Had Shawn blacked out? And had some good fortune saved his life by putting a tree in the way? And making Cherry so bright as to remember a single simple statement. It showed how much what he said meant to her!

It took a few minutes to get through to Madeleine. She listened in silence before answering.

'St. Ives? Where's that? Cornwall? At the hospital? Thank you, Simon. You'll be going down? Yes, so will I. But immediately.'

'It might not be wise at this stage,' Simon said. 'I think we should consult his doctor. When Shawn recovers consciousness . . .'

'He must see me,' Madeleine said triumphantly. 'Then he will be happy and all will be well.' She rang off before he could speak.

Next, Simon called the hospital in St. Ives. It took even longer to reach Dr. Miles. He sounded annoyed.

'Slight concussion, I'd say. Obviously other troubles but they are not immediately important.'

'Should I come down? I mean, could I help?'

'You could not,' Dr. Miles snapped. 'All this publicity is bad enough. Already we've got reporters here. How the news gets around, I can't think. In any case, his girl friend is here . . .'

'There's just one thing, Dr. Miles. I'm rather worried because a girl who says my brother is her fiancé is on her way down to see him.'

'I see . . . you said *a girl who says . . .?*'

'M'm. The thing is that my brother told me about her and, so I gathered, has no intention of marrying her. His interests are elsewhere.'

'So I gathered from this girl,' Dr. Miles said dryly. 'Unless all girls make this up. What you mean is that it might be unwise for your brother, on recovering consciousness, to be faced by this girl from London. Right?'

'Right. She is extremly emotional and could create a scene. Well, maybe I shouldn't interfere but I'd rather she didn't see him at once. I'd prefer him to know she was *there,* not to let her just walk in.'

'I get you. You'll be coming down?'

'As soon as I can be of help.' He gave his Hastings phone number. 'We're pretty chaotic at the moment but . . .'

Dr. Miles laughed. 'Aren't we all. Don't worry about your brother, though, his girl friend will look after him.' He laughed again.

Simon went straight to Charing Cross and was lucky enough to catch a train quickly. Then he remembered Aunt Flo. Surely Cherry would ring her to tell her all was well? Or nearly well.

The train seemed to crawl even though it was rushing along, shaking like mad. The countryside flashed by, beautiful in the sunshine, with the contented cows lying down on the grass, and the still quiet villages looking peaceful.

But all Simon thought of was Cherry. How worried she must have been. What a shock to find Shawn unconscious in the car that could so easily have gone over the cliff and into the sea, far below.

Poor Shawn. Where cars were concerned he seemed fated. He would have to listen to the specialists and remain patiently in bed for six months. Cherry would look after him . . .

Funny. Simon lit a cigarette. He saw an elderly woman scowling at him, looked round and saw *No Smoking* signs everywhere, so put out the cigarette and the old woman smiled. As once he could not forget Alicia, now it was Cherry who haunted his thoughts. No matter what he began to think about, it would end in Cherry. The way she smiled. Her laugh. Why did he have to fall in love?

CHAPTER FIFTEEN

It was getting late by the time Simon parked his car and made his way to Aunt Flo's flat. It had been a hard working afternoon and evening but he felt he had to see her, to reassure her about Shawn. Phones were inadequate as regards that sort of thing.

A wet summer's evening but a calm sea, he

thought as he waited after he had rung the bell.

He had a shock when the door was opened for he had expected to see Teresa there. Instead it was Cherry.

'But I thought . . .' he began.

'Come in. Aunt Flo will be thrilled. Let me take your mac . . .'

'I thought you were in Cornwall . . .' he said as he took off his macintosh and gave it to her.

'I was . . .'

'Who is it, dear? You have got the loose chain on?' Aunt Flo called.

Simon went through to the small sitting-room. 'Aunt Flo . . .'

'Dear boy . . .' she held out her arms. 'What a lovely evening. Shawn found safe and sound, Cherry calling in to see me and now you.'

'I came to tell you about Shawn . . .' Simon began but Aunt Flo was looking at her watch.

'Switch on the telly, dear boy, will you? When Cherry phoned your doctor friend to say all was well, he told her you would be on T.V. tonight. He even found the time and it should be any moment now . . . Cherry, Cherry . . .' she called.

Simon sank into a deep armchair and groaned. 'Who wants to look at me?'

Cherry brought in a tray of coffee 'I do . . .' she said with a smile.

'Well, I don't. I was tricked into it.' As they waited for the picture to develop before them, he told them briefly of Madeleine's note and his shocked amazement when he walked in and found the cameras. 'I expect they've cut most of it . . .'

He sat silently as they watched. It was short. Mostly shots of Madeleine, showing her beautiful long legs, her affectionate grasp of Simon's arm, the way they sat together on the couch, Madeleine leaning against him.

'She's very pretty,' Cherry said, her voice odd.

'I look ghastly . . .' Simon moaned.

'I think you look very handsome, dear lad . . .'

All were silent as Madeleine spoke again. Simon closed his eyes as he heard her voice.

'No two men kiss alike. I should know. Every woman knows. But Shawn, he kisses so . . . how shall I express myself? So warmly, so excitingly . . .'

Simon shivered. This must be awful for Cherry, He opened his eyes in time to see Madeleine hugging herself, laughing up at him. He was sitting, looking pompous and uncomfortable on the couch by her side.

'Simon!' Madeleine's voice came clearly, scornfully.

'He didn't even kiss me. It was like kissing a stone.'

Simon wanted to rush and switch off the wretched television set but Aunt Flo was leaning forward, her face intent as she watched.

'You don't like kissing girls, Dr. Britten?' the interviewer asked silkily.

And the stodgy miserable-looking man sitting by the side of a beautiful girl said quietly: 'I only kiss the girls I love.'

That was the end of Simon, apparently, for after that there were enlargements of photos of Shawn, compared with the photo they'd taken of Simon as he entered the room and stood there, looking stunned and horrified.

It was obvious that Madeleine was thoroughly enjoying herself. It was a relief to Simon when it was over and Aunt Flo told them to switch off.

'It wasn't too bad, dear lad,' Aunt Flo tried to comfort him.

'Too bad? It was ghastly. Just think how I'll be teased tomorrow!'

'I think you behaved very well,' Cherry said. 'After all, you'd had no warning.'

He looked at her gratefully. 'I must say it was a shock.'

Cherry tried not to smile. 'That was pretty obvious.'

The phone bell shrilled. 'I'll answer it, Aunt Flo,' Cherry added and hurried to the hall where the phone was on a stand with a stool part of it.

'What . . . no? yes . . . Oh, I say. Wish I'd been there . . . No . . . ?'

Simon sat still, looking miserably at his hands. Cherry was being very brave about the whole thing. How could she have left Shawn, though? Had it been because she knew Madeleine was going down to see him? Had Shawn, at sometime perhaps confessed his love for Madeleine and that he was going to marry her after all? That could be the only explanation . . .

Cherry came hurrying back, she stood in the doorway, cheeks flushed, eyes shining. 'Shawn's all right. He's regained consciousness and remembers everything. He was driving along the cliff and then everything went went black. He knew nothing more. Madeleine's been down . . .' She began to laugh. 'Oh, I wish I'd been there. Apparently Madeleine insisted on seeing him and Shawn refused to but in the end Teresa persuaded him to . . .'

'Teresa?' Simon said slowly. 'Where does she come into this?'

Cherry looked amused. 'Surely you knew? When I came over and told Aunt Flo and Teresa that I remembered Shawn saying once he wanted to go to Carbis Bay to see where his mother had lived, Teresa and I decided to drive down at once. We did and we found the car and . . . well, I left her there.'

'But couldn't she have driven back to tell Aunt Flo? I mean, you had to come by train, besides, didn't you want to stay with Shawn?' Simon said slowly, trying to work things out that puzzled him.

Cherry came into the room to curl up in an

armchair.

'Gosh, Simon, sometimes you amaze me. D'you mean you didn't *know*?'

'Know what?'

'That Shawn had a crush on Teresa and she an even worse one on him . . .'

Simon stared at her, horrified. Why, this was even worse than before. 'Teresa and Shawn . . .?'

Cherry nodded. 'Of course. Ideal for one another. Both needing someone to fuss over. I don't know if you knew but Teresa was a nurse at one time before she nursed her mother, so she understands and she'll handle Shawn perfectly.'

'I still don't get it though I'm trying.' Simon looked at Aunt Flo. 'Did you know all this?'

'I didn't *know* but I guessed, dear boy. When Teresa began getting books about Australia and talking about emigrating I had a suspicion. Then the way Shawn behaved . . . well, I began to think he *was* serious. I know he was very worried about something but after he told Teresa, it didn't seem to worry him.'

'He told her about his health?'

Cherry chimed in. 'He told her everything. His fear, the tests, his constant blackouts, the fact that he couldn't always remember what he had done and he was never sure if others were kidding him or not. He said the specialist had said the trouble could be cured. It meant six months in bed and special treatment.' She smiled. 'He must love Teresa an awful lot for he can talk to her.' The smile vanished and her voice was sad as she added: 'Some men seem unable to talk.'

'And you think Shawn will stay in bed for six months and have treatment?'

Cherry looked at Simon. 'I don't think. I know Shawn would do anything for Teresa . . .'

Simon felt an almost irresistible desire to take Cherry in his arms. How could she treat it so casually? What a fine actress she must be, what self-control when her heart must be broken.

'And Madeleine, Cherry?' Aunt Flo asked eagerly.

'Well, Teresa told Shawn he couldn't run away from Madeleine for ever and she would back him up, so Madeleine was allowed in, and Shawn said 'You know it's all over so why put on an act? It's been over for ages. You ruined it and now I'm marrying the love of my life . . .' and, you'll never believe this, Simon, Shawn kissed Teresa's hand.'

'Good for him,' Aunt Flo said. 'A little gallantry can never hurt. So what did Madeleine do?'

'She glared at him, then at Teresa and said "I'm sorry for *you*" and dashed out of the ward.'

Aunt Flo chuckled. 'So that was that. Shawn is freed only to be hooked by Teresa.'

'I think she'll make him a wonderful wife,'

Cherry said.

Simon looked at her. His brave Cherry, hiding her broken heart.

'Simon dear boy,' Aunt Flo said. 'I wonder if you'd go into my bedroom and get my glasses. I think they're on the dressing table, but they may be in the drawer by my bed, or on the table by the window.'

'I'll go . . .' Cherry began.

Aunt Flo frowned. 'No. You must be tired after all that travelling. Let Simon go . . .'

He stood up, towering above them. 'Of course.'

It took some time looking for the glasses. They were neither on the dressing-table or the table, nor were they in the drawer. He went back. 'I'm sorry but I can't find them . . .'

'Oh dear . . . I must have put them down somewhere.' Aunt Flo rose. 'I'll just have to look . . .'

'I'm sure they're not in there . . .'

'Then they may be in the kitchen,' Aunt Flo said and left the room, pulling the door behind her.

Cherry stood up. Simon stared at her, as he searched for the right words. 'I am sorry, Cherry, about . . .' he began but stopped for, with a scream, she leapt into his arms and somehow they had closed round her tightly.

'It was a mouse, Simon . . . a mouse . . .' she cried.

He laughed. 'Nothing to be afraid of . . .'

'I'm terrified of them.' She clung tightly to him.

Their faces were close. It seemed the most natural thing in the world to do so he did it.

He kissed her.

It was a long satisfying kiss. Satisfying and amazing because of her response.

She moved her head away, looking up into his eyes.

'You said you only kiss girls you love. Does that mean?'

'That I love you?' Simon's arms tightened round her. 'Yes, it does. I always have but . . .'

'You were afraid?'

'I didn't want to catch you on the rebound . . .'

'No, Simon,' she said gently, 'that wasn't your fear. You'd been rejected twice. By your father and Alicia. You were afraid I'd reject you.' She looked up at him anxiously: 'Aren't I right, Simon?'

He caught his breath. 'You know, I think you are right. I kept telling myself that even if you said No, it wouldn't be final.'

'But you knew you couldn't bear the pain of a third No. What made you think I'd say No?'

'Well . . .' Everything was a bit muzzy. He kept wanting to kiss her yet she went on talking. What did this all mean? Could it . . .? Dared he hope it meant . . . what he hoped it meant! 'Well, you weren't exactly friendly, you know. You told me I was spoiled . . .'

'And you were. Or you *had* to believe you

210

were and this is where Aunt Flo helped you. Go on . . .'

'Then you never ever stopped talking about Shawn.'

Cherry smiled. 'I wanted to make you jealous.'

'I was but . . .'

'You're the type that curls up in shell when hurt. Why didn't you tell me?'

'Because every time I tried to something interrupted us or you misunderstood me . . . Cherry what are you trying to tell me? Are you being kind and all that . . .'

'Not in the least,' she said, her voice sharp. 'I've been trying to make you tell me you loved me for ages. A girl can't accept a man until he asks her. At least, maybe some girls can but I can't, I have to use devious means. You do love me?'

He kissed her. Again. And again. 'Does that answer your question?'

'A girl still needs to be told.'

'Cherry Corfield,' he said solemnly. 'I love you.'

She smiled. 'Dr. Simon Britten. I love you . . .' He went to kiss her again but she dodged him. Then moved out of his arms. 'Simon, I think if our marriage is to be a success, I should tell the truth. Just a moment . . .'

She bent down and picked up something from the floor. Then held out her hand. On the palm, lay a small mouse. Not a live mouse

211

or a dead one, but a knitted mouse.

Simon stared at it. 'You tricked me . . . you hussy.' He burst out laughing and grabbed her but again, she avoided him. 'You . . .'

'It was really Aunt Flo's idea. She said you were like a tortoise and even tortoises need a little help now and then. So I thought if I gave you a little push . . .'

'Little push! You nearly knocked me over when you jumped at me.'

'Did you mind, Simon?' She was dodging round the chairs as he pretended to chase her.

'Mind? I loved every moment of it. Like to do it again?' He held out his arms invitingly.

She moved towards him and he caught her hand, bent and kissed it. 'A little gallantry as Aunt Flo said . . .'

The door opened and Aunt Flo stood there, a smile making her eyes sparkle, her face looking happy.

'Have you finished yet?' she asked. 'I found my glasses.'

'Finished?' Simon said. 'Why, we've only just begun.'